THE GREEK'S
PREGNANT
CINDERELLA

THE GREEK'S PREGNANT CINDERELLA

MICHELLE SMART

MILLS & BOON

First published in Great Britain 2019
by Mills & Boon, an imprint of HarperCollins*Publishers*
1 London Bridge Street, London, SE1 9GF

Large Print edition 2019

© 2019 Michelle Smart

ISBN: 978-0-263-08293-7

MIX
Paper from
responsible sources
FSC® C007454

This book is produced from independently certified FSC™ paper to ensure responsible forest management. For more information visit www.harpercollins.co.uk/green.

Printed and bound in Great Britain
by CPI Group (UK) Ltd, Croydon, CR0 4YY

CHAPTER ONE

TABITHA BRIGSTOCK WHEELED her trolley to the laundry room and heaved the sack of dirty linen and towels from the suites she'd spent the morning cleaning into the white dirty washing tub, then left the laundry to wheel the trolley further up the corridor to the storage room, where she locked it away with the other trollies. Her hands were red and sore but there was no time to go to her room to rub the hand lotion on them that sometimes stopped them cracking too badly. The staff quarters were right at the other end of the hotel, a good fifteen-minute walk away.

Instead she climbed the stairs and headed to the far end of the first floor. She knocked on the door out of habit then used her master key to unlock it.

'Hi, Mrs Coulter,' she said cheerfully as she walked into the opulent suite. 'How are you feeling? Sorry I couldn't pop in earlier but they needed me to help out on the second floor.'

At eighty-three, Mrs Coulter was the oldest guest at Vienna's Basinas Palace Hotel and had been in residence for three months. The poor woman had been floored by a virus that had left her bed-bound for two weeks. Tabitha had been very concerned and had taken to dropping in on her regularly to make sure she was okay. Thankfully, Mrs Coulter had been much improved the last couple of days, and today she was up and dressed and eating her lunch at the table by the window that overlooked the palace's vast grounds.

Mrs Coulter smiled, the twinkle in her eye that had been missing all week very much back. 'I'm feeling much better, thank you. And thank you for getting Melanie to check on me earlier.'

'Not a problem. I've got the vitamins you asked for.' She pulled the small plastic pot out of her handbag and put it on the table.

Gnarled arthritic hands covered hers. 'You are an angel. Will you sit and have a cup of tea with me?'

As Tabitha still had twenty minutes of her lunch break left, she took the offered seat and poured them both a cup from the bone-china pot.

It felt wonderful to sit after six straight hours

of physical exertion. The hotel was in a state of great excitement. The Greek owner, Giannis Basinas, was hosting a masquerade ball there that evening for the world's elite.

Tabitha had caught a glimpse of him earlier. She'd just finished cleaning a room and was wheeling her trolley down the corridor when he'd strolled past. Her heart had soared to see him but, as normal, he didn't spare her so much as a glance.

In the five months since she'd started working there, she had seen the billionaire widower, who was rumoured to be descended from Greek royalty, only a handful of times. The Basinas Palace Hotel was but a small part of his vast empire. When he did bother to show his face in Vienna, the excitement and fear amongst the staff was palpable. The hotel had once been a royal palace and was now regarded as Europe's most prestigious hotel with a price tag to match. Working there was a coup in itself but, should standards be deemed to have dropped, the risk of being fired was all too real.

Tabitha could not afford to lose her job and had no idea what it was about Giannis that meant every rare glimpse of him played on her mind so much or made her stomach come alive with butterflies. As a live-in member of staff, to be fired would be to be made homeless. The salary here was much better than her old job in a small English hotel, and the tips were often amazing, but even with all the overtime she grabbed she still hadn't saved anywhere near enough for a deposit on her own home.

That was all she wanted. A place of her own. A home where she could be safe. A home that no one could ever take away from her.

'I was hoping you would come see me this lunchtime,' Mrs Coulter said.

Tabitha raised an eyebrow. 'Are you ready for a game of cards?' The two women had taken to playing rummy most days when Tabitha's day shift was over.

'My head's still too fuzzy for that, my dear. No, I wanted to discuss tonight's ball.'

'The masquerade ball?'

'Is there another one I should know about?'

Tabitha laughed. 'I hope not. I'm grateful for the extra shifts it's giving me but I'd need a holiday to recoup if we had another one too soon.' And she could not afford a holiday.

The twinkle reappeared in Mrs Coulter's eye. 'I have a ticket for it.'

'No way!' Tickets for the ball were forty-thousand euros. To have the privilege of forking out that astronomical amount of money, you had to be invited. To be invited, you had to be rich and part of the global elite. It was an open secret that all the single women who'd been invited were under the age of thirty, the rumour—not denied—being that Giannis Basinas was using the ball as a means of finding himself a new wife. Mrs Coulter was rich and recently widowed but she was not part of the global elite and she absolutely was not under the age of thirty. 'How did you get that?'

Mrs Coulter winked and tapped her nose. 'A lady has her secrets, dear.'

Tabitha felt a surge of excitement for her. To go to the ball... She'd seen all the preparations for it, heard all the whispered talk, and it was obvious it was going to be the ball of century. 'Do you want me to do your hair and nails for it? My shift finishes at four, so I'll have time...'

'No, dear. The ticket is for you.'

'Sorry?'

'I bought the ticket for *you*.'

Tabitha was momentarily struck dumb. She stared at the wizened old woman with the white wispy hair and twinkling eyes and wondered when she'd gained such an evil sense of humour. It had to be a joke. Who would spend forty-thousand euros on a ticket to a ball for a chambermaid?

The gnarled hand covered hers again. 'Tabitha,' she said earnestly. 'You have been a godsend to me. You have looked after me since I first arrived in Vienna and often in your own personal time. You've cared for me this week when my own selfish children could hardly be bothered to call to see if I was okay. You work your fingers to the bone for little money and you never complain. You're a ray of sunshine in a dark world and I wanted to show my love and appreciation for all that you do.'

Tabitha swallowed. A ray of sunshine? Her?

The only people who had ever said such nice things to her had been her father and paternal grandmother. Her lovely grandmother had died when she'd been seven but her memories of her were strong. Mrs Coulter had the same mischievous twinkle her grandmother had had and the same easy affection. Tabitha supposed that was what had drawn her to the elderly lady to begin with and partly why she felt such deep affection for her.

'The ticket is in my name. Tonight, you will be Amelia Coulter, and you will dance with handsome men and drink champagne and spend an evening being who you were born to be.'

Tabitha blinked, partly to push back the tears threatening to spill down her face and partly in shock.

Being who you were born to be...?

She had spent the past four years trying her hardest to forget her birth right. The memories were too painful. All she could do was tackle each day as it came and look to the future.

Her heart thumped. Did Mrs Coulter know...?

The twinkling eyes were steady on hers. If Mrs Coulter knew Tabitha's true identity, she was keeping her cards close to her chest.

But Tabitha had never hidden her true self. Her name was the only thing her stepmother had been unable to take from her. She'd taken everything else, though. Her home, her education, her money, her future...

'Take a look in my wardrobe. Go on, dear.'

On legs that felt strangely drugged, Tabitha stepped through to the bedroom.

'Right-hand door,' Mrs Coulter called.

'What am I looking for?'

'You'll see.'

And she did see.

When she opened the right-hand door of the wardrobe, all that hung on the rail was a floor-length ball gown that could have leapt off the pages of a fairy tale.

She stretched out a hand and ran her fingers over the delicate material, her eyes soaking up the pastel-pale pinks and greens overlaid with embellished gold-threaded patterns and en-crusted with jewels and the palest of pink roses. An eighteenth-century princess would have been thrilled to wear something so beautiful.

On the shelf above it lay a pair of white-gold high-heeled shoes, a white eye-mask with gold detailing and gold braiding around its edges and a plume of wispy pale pink feathers shaped into a flower on the left cheek.

Hands now shaking, she took hold of a shoe and examined it in awe.

It was her size.

Dazed, she went back to the living area of the suite. 'How…?'

Mrs Coulter smiled. 'A lady has her ways.'

'I can't. I wish…' She took a deep breath and hugged the shoe to her chest. 'I wish I could go but I can't. If I get caught, I'll be fired. We've all been warned.' And warned unambiguously. Any member of staff caught trying to enter the ball would have their contract of employment terminated.

But Mrs Coulter was not to be deterred. 'We will make you unrecognisable. No one will know it's you—no one will be expecting you to be there. In my experience, people see what they want and expect to see. They will not see a chambermaid. Come back here at five. I've arranged for a beautician to join us. She will turn you into a princess. And then tomorrow you can join me for lunch and tell me all about it.' She gave a tinkle of laughter. 'I admit, I'm not being entirely altruistic. I'm too old and my knees too shot to go to the ball myself but I can live it vicariously through you.'

Hot tears prickled the back of Tabitha's eyes. No one had ever done such a thing for her before.

'Do not be afraid, my dear. Tonight you will

be a princess and you will go to the ball, and I will not hear another word of argument about it.'

Giannis Basinas left the apartment he used as a base when in Vienna and strolled up the rose-hedged path that led to his hotel. He could have earmarked one of the suites for his own use but he preferred to give himself at least an illusion of privacy. Privacy was a concept frequently ignored by his large, exuberant family.

It was partly down to his family that he was making this walk now dressed in an all-black, leather swallowtail suit and hosting this masquerade ball. His sisters had been dropping hints since he'd turned thirty-five that he needed to find a new wife. He'd come to the reluctant conclusion that they were right.

When his oldest friend Alessio Palvetti had pulled in a favour owed from their school days and asked him to host a masquerade ball, using a specific event team to manage it, Giannis had figured the ball could work in his favour. He could repay his debt *and* let his sisters believe he was serious about finding a wife. Everyone would be happy.

He didn't hold much hope that his ideal woman

would emerge tonight but this was as good an opportunity to find her as any. He'd even let Niki, his youngest sister and the biggest social-ite in his family, select fifty of the four hundred guests to invite. These fifty guests were unmar-ried women, their wealth determined by their ability to pay the forty-thousand-euro price tag he'd set the tickets at.

If Giannis was going to marry again, he had three criteria. Firstly, and most importantly, his potential wife had to be independently rich. He would not make the same mistake as he'd made in his first marriage. Secondly, she must be of childbearing age, a criterion that was self-explanatory. Thirdly, and least importantly, she must be pleasant to look at. She didn't have to be a model, or even be particularly beautiful, but if he was going to spend the rest of his life with one woman he would prefer it to be with some-one he found attractive.

Slipping through a rear door into the hotel he'd bought less than two years ago, he made his way to the ballroom.

Giannis's business interests were varied but mostly concentrated in shipping and property across the globe. This former palace he'd spent millions on renovating into a world-class hotel was his first venture into the tourism industry outside his Greek home. As a status symbol, there was none better.

About to open a side door into the ballroom, he spotted a female guest on the cantilevered stairs. Her fingers trailed the railing as she made her descent. Her other hand clutched the gold invitation all ball guests were required to show on their arrival.

There was something hesitant about her graceful walk that made him look twice.

He looked at her. Then looked again.

Although much of her face was hidden behind a white-gold eye-mask with a plume of dusky-pink feathers on the left cheek, there was something about her that set his pulses racing.

He couldn't tear his eyes away.

Her beautiful dress, all delicate pale greens, dusky pinks, golds and jewels that sparkled when the light caught them, was strapless and form-fitting to the waist then puffed out to fall in layers to her hidden feet.

She looked like a princess.

She could *be* a princess.

He imagined the dazzling circle the skirt of the dress would make on the dance floor...

Leaving the door he'd been about to enter, he approached her as she reached the bottom of the stairs.

She was shorter than he'd thought and, up close, even more ravishing. Honey-blonde hair had been coiled into an elegant knot at the base of a graceful neck adorned with a gold choker necklace covered in jewels, and roses that matched her dress and the drop earrings hanging from the lobes of her pretty ears.

She was the most exquisite creature he had ever set eyes on.

'You look lost,' he said in English.

A pair of cornflower-blue eyes met his from behind the mask.

Full, heart-shaped lips curved into a hesitant smile.

'Do you need directions to the room the guests are meeting in? Or are you waiting for someone?' She wore a glimmering diamond on her right hand but there was no ring on her left.

She shook her head in obvious shyness.

'You don't need directions or you're not waiting for someone?' Or did she not understand him? It was a rare event to meet someone in his world who did not speak English.

When she finally spoke, her cut-glass English accent contained a huskiness to it. 'I'm not waiting for anyone.'

Better and better.

He held an arm out to her. 'Then allow me to escort you, Miss...'

'Tabitha.' Colour stained what he could see of her cheeks. 'My name is Tabitha.'

'A pleasure to meet you, Tabitha. I'm Giannis Basinas and it would be my pleasure if you would allow me to escort you to the ball.'

Tabitha could have screamed at her stupidity. *Why* had she given him her real name?

She hadn't even reached the ballroom yet and already she'd blown her cover. And with Giannis Basinas of all people!

She was supposed to be Amelia Coulter, the name on the invitation in her hand.

She should have turned Mrs Coulter's incredibly generous offer down but she'd been caught up in the moment, her head turned by the beautiful dress, her heart aching for one night, just one night, of freedom from the unrelenting drudgery of a life spent scrubbing bathrooms and cleaning rooms.

This was the sort of ball at which, if her father had lived, she could have been a real guest. She would have been here by right, not deception.

If Giannis suspected for a moment that she was a lowly hotel employee she would be fired on the spot.

But there was no hint of recognition.

But then, he'd never looked at her before. And why would he? He employed hundreds of people at this hotel alone. Chambermaids came bottom of the pecking order, a faceless army who flitted unobtrusively through the corridors and cleaned the rich guests' rooms.

The thought calmed her a little but it was with a heart that raced that she slipped her hand through his offered arm, then found it racing even harder.

Tall, with dark brown hair cut short at the sides and long at the top, Giannis had a nose that was too long and his chin was a little too pointed for him to be considered traditionally handsome. But there was something about him, whether it was the high cheekbones, the clear blue eyes or the full bottom lip, that drew attention.

It had drawn her attention from her first glance.

His was a face that had lived and had the lines etched in his forehead and around the eyes to prove it.

He might not be traditionally handsome but in the black leather swallowtail suit and black leather eye-mask he wore as his masquerade costume, which gave him an almost piratical air, he was devastating.

'Which part of England are you from?' he asked as they strolled down a wide corridor.

'Oxfordshire,' she answered cautiously.

'A beautiful county.'

It was, she thought wistfully. She'd avoided the entire county since she'd been thrown out of her home. It hurt too much to think of everything she'd lost and everything she missed.

However, she smiled, nodded her agreement and prayed for a change to the conversation.

What would be even better would be an increase to the pace Giannis had set. They were walking so slowly a tortoise could have overtaken them.

Her mind raced as to how she could slip away from him before she had to hand over the invitation written in the name of a woman who was not Tabitha.

If she had left Mrs Coulter's room a minute earlier or later she wouldn't have bumped into the one person she'd really needed to avoid.

'I went to university in Oxford,' he said. 'Boarding school at Quilton House in Wiltshire. Do you know it?'

That explained his flawless English.

'I know of it.' Quilton House was one of the oldest schools in the world and certainly the most expensive. Only the filthy rich could afford to send their children there. A few of her school friends' brothers had attended it.

'What school did you go to?' he asked.

'Beddingdales.'

He laughed, a deep, rumbly sound that played melodically in her ears. 'My first girlfriend went to Beddingdales. I would ask if you knew her, but I suspect you're a lot younger than me.'

'Probably.'

He laughed even louder. 'You don't waste words, do you?'

'I'm sorry, I didn't mean…'

He stopped walking and fixed clear blue eyes on hers. 'Don't apologise. Honesty is a rare, refreshing trait in this world we live in.'

They reached the door that led into the area

where the guests were to wait before the ball was declared open. In a moment she would have to hand over the invitation for her name to be confirmed on the guest list.

Her heart pounded.

She needed to slip away.

Before she could think of an excuse to flee, Giannis took hold of the hand tucked into his arm and brought it to his lips. His eyes sparkled as he razed the lightest of kisses against the knuckles. 'I have a couple of things I need to check on before the ball starts. I will find you.'

Then he bowed his head and turned on his heel, leaving nothing but the scent of his spicy cologne in his wake.

Tabitha slowly released the breath she'd been holding and closed her eyes.

Her heart still pounded, although whether that was an effect of the kiss on her hand or the close call she'd just had she couldn't determine.

'Are you coming in, miss?'

The uniformed guard had opened the door for her.

She swallowed.

It wasn't too late. She didn't have to do this.

But then she caught sight of a waiter holding a

tray of champagne and the longing in her heart overshadowed the fear.

She could stay for one glass of champagne, she reasoned. That couldn't do any harm. One glass of champagne and then, when the ball was declared open, slip away and return to her room and the safe anonymity of her servile life.

But she would have one glass of champagne first.

She stepped into a small holding room. Another uniformed guard stood on the other side of the door, a large tablet in his hand. Her heart almost stopped.

She recognised him. She'd spoken to him numerous times in the staff room.

There was not a flicker of recognition in his returning stare.

He greeted her with a polite smile. 'May I see your invitation please, miss?'

Hoping he didn't notice the tremor in her hand, she passed it to him.

He peered at it closely then turned his attention to his tablet until he found her name on the list. He pressed his finger to it then smiled again at her and nodded at the double doors at the other side of the room. 'Guests are assembling through that door. Enjoy your evening, Miss Coulter.'

Air rushed out of her lungs.

Mrs Coulter had been right. The dress and the mask acted as the perfect disguise.

'Thank you,' she murmured.

Straightening her back, Tabitha held her head high. Yet another doorman opened the double doors for her to step through.

The noise she was greeted with from the reception room made her blink. The guests already congregated were in high spirits. Laughter and the buzz of excited chatter filled the air, melding with the music coming from the corner, where a pianist was playing a familiar tune.

She soaked up all of this in the time it took to step over the threshold.

A waitress holding a tray of champagne approached her.

Tabitha took a flute with a smile and restrained herself from tipping the contents down her throat in one swallow.

Whatever the circumstances of her life now, she'd been raised to be a lady. Ladies did not tip drinks down their necks.

She brought the flute to her mouth and took a small sip.

The explosion of bubbles in her mouth was enough to make her want to cry.

Only twice in her life had she tasted champagne. The first time had been at her father's wedding when she'd been ten. The second had been when she'd been fourteen. Her stepmother had thrown an eighteenth birthday party for Fiona, the oldest of Tabitha's stepsisters. The party had been an elaborate affair with no expense spared.

The celebrations for Tabitha's own eighteenth birthday had been markedly different. Her stepmother had celebrated by throwing Tabitha out of the family home.

The big wide world she'd looked forward to embracing had shrunk overnight.

Any alcohol she'd consumed since then had been whatever was cheapest. No Freshers' Week at university for her. While her school friends had scattered to various higher education institutions around the country—the majority intent on having a fantastic three years getting drunk and attending the odd lecture when they could fit it in their busy social schedules—Tabitha had already been gaining callouses on her hands from working as a cleaner in the small family-owned hotel. The pay had been terrible but the job had come with accommodation.

The call for silence broke through her sad reminiscences.

The master of ceremonies greeted the four hundred guests and then, with a flourish, declared the masquerade ball open.

CHAPTER TWO

CAUGHT IN THE tide of bodies, Tabitha entered the enormous ballroom.

Her hand flew to her throat as she took in the lavish transformation the already opulent room had undergone.

From the grand high ceiling hung balloons of gold, silver and white, the walls lined with heavy drapes following the colour theme. In the far corner sat the champagne fountain the staff had been talking about for days.

Everything glittered. Everything shone, especially the colourful, fabulously dressed guests.

It was like entering a magical wonderland and Tabitha's heart ached at the beauty of it.

She finished her champagne, placed the empty flute on the tray of a passing waiter and took her place amongst the ladies forming a long line to the left of the springy wooden dance floor.

The gentlemen lined up on the right and then the orchestra struck the first note of the first tune.

Four ballet dancers appeared and performed a short but exquisite dance for them. No sooner had they danced out of the ballroom to rapturous applause than two-dozen professional ballroom dancers, notable for the ladies' all-white gowns and the gentlemen's traditional black tail suits, took to the floor and performed the first waltz.

It had been a long time since Tabitha's ballroom dancing lessons at school. It was the one lesson every pupil had looked forward to and she'd been no exception. She'd never imagined then that she would have to wait so long to put the moves she'd learned into practice.

These dancers were incredible and the whispers around her indicated there were world champions amongst them.

Yet she found her gaze darting over the line of gentlemen on the other side of the room.

She shouldn't be looking for him, she scolded herself. Hoping that his words about finding her were true was nothing but a fool's wish, and a dangerous one at that. If Giannis discovered she was an employee, she would lose everything.

And, even if he had meant it, there were one-hundred and ninety-nine other women here, most of them far more attractive than she was.

He'd probably forgotten her already.

The professional dancers finished their waltz and then came the words Tabitha had once longed to hear in a setting just like this, and not from a school mistress: *'Alles Walzer!'*

Everyone dance!

The gentlemen set off towards the ladies.

Excitement surged inside her.

For so many years she had dreamed of this moment, yet for so many she'd stopped believing it could happen.

She didn't even care that the gentleman making a beeline towards her was old enough to be her father and short enough to fit in her handbag.

When he was only a couple of feet from her, his path was suddenly blocked by another, much taller and broader figure who seemed to appear from nowhere.

Her heart stopped then, after a breathless pause, kick-started back to life with fury.

Giannis stood before her, his head tilted, a gleam in his eyes as bright as the chandeliers hanging amidst the balloons above them.

'Darf ich bitten?'

The traditional way of asking a lady to dance at a Viennese Ball.

The very words Tabitha had once dreamed of hearing.

She stared into the clear blue eyes, the strangest of feelings forming in her veins.

Her knees sank into a curtsey without any input from her brain.

Strong nostrils flared. He put a hand to his stomach and inclined his head in a bow.

Then he took hold of her right hand with his left and slipped his other hand around her waist to rest just above the small of her back.

Sensation shot through the fingers being held in his, seeping straight into her bloodstream.

Muscle memory took control of Tabitha's left hand and she placed it on his right bicep, splaying the thumb away from her fingers to cup it.

The orchestra struck the first note and then she was being spun across the great ballroom in his arms.

In Giannis Basinas's arms.

Her first ever dance with a man.

This man.

This man who controlled their moves effortlessly and steered them around the other couples without his clear blue eyes ever leaving hers.

She couldn't tear her gaze from the face that

had captured her attention from that very first glance either.

And nor could she stop herself breathing in his spicy scent.

But, even with the feeling that she had entered the most magical of dreams strong inside her, there was a voice in her head whispering that this one dance was all she could have with him.

Never mind the danger that being with him put her in, he would want to dance with other women. If the rumours were true and this ball was a ruse for him to find a new wife then he would want to spread himself out and talk and dance with as many women as he could.

It felt as if no time had passed at all when the dance finished. The couples around them parted like the Red Sea.

Tabitha let out a breath that contained both relief and disappointment and moved her hand from his arm. But there was no relinquishing her hand by his. His grip on it tightened.

He brought his mouth to her ear. 'You don't think I'm letting you go, do you?'

Brand new sensation skittered down her skin at the warmth of his breath on her ear and cheek.

She tried to think of an excuse to pull away but her brain refused to co-operate.

Her body refused to co-operate too. Her hand reached back up to cup his bicep.

Around them, new couples formed.

The orchestra played the first note of the next dance and then she was being spun around the floor again.

All the reasons she needed to escape seeped away as the music made its way through her body and down into her dancing feet. Masked faces floated around her, dresses twirled, beautifully played music...

And the heavenly arms of Giannis Basinas.

When that dance finished and the master of ceremonies took to the floor to announce that it was time to dance the polonaise, she met Giannis's eyes. There was a question in them.

She nodded. She remembered this dance.

He smiled and, holding her left hand, led her to the forming line of couples.

In and out they wove, separating then coming back together, curtseying, separating... She curtsied and danced with other men but her attention was always on Giannis.

She simply could not tear her gaze from him.

Not until they'd danced another waltz, and then a foxtrot, did he steer her away from the dance floor to one of the round tables on the raised dais running the lengths of the ballroom walls with a murmured, 'Time for a drink.'

Unwilling to leave her side for a moment, Giannis signalled for champagne to be brought to them.

He had a feeling this ravishing creature would disappear if he turned his back on her.

She hadn't exchanged one word with him during their time on the dance floor.

Their champagne was brought to them. He held his flute to hers then drank from it. 'Are you hungry?'

She shook her head.

'You don't speak much, do you?' he observed. In his experience, women always had to fill any silence with chatter, however inane. His sisters were the worst for it. Their mother always said Niki had been born with a never-ending battery in her tongue. He'd caught a glimpse of Niki in the arms of a bemused man trying to cut above her incessant chatter to waltz her around the dance floor.

Slim shoulders raised in a tiny shrug. 'I do if I have something to say.'

He laughed. 'And do you have anything to say, Tabitha?'

She shook her head again.

'I thought Beddingdales taught its girls how to make small talk in social situations.'

There was the faintest spark of amusement in the cornflower eyes. 'I failed that class.'

He laughed. 'But obviously not the ballroom-dancing lessons.'

'I liked those.'

'Do you go to many balls?'

Another shake of the head.

'I'm going to have to stop asking you closed questions, aren't I?'

Now there was the slightest of curves in the full heart-shaped lips to accompany her shaking head.

He laughed. 'Tell me about yourself.'

The faint amusement he'd detected vanished. She looked away from him, her lips pulling in together. 'What do you want to know?'

Everything.

'Let us start with how old you are.'

'Twenty-two.'

That surprised him. The features he could see beneath the mask covering her face indicated youth but the way she carried herself suggested someone older.

'Have you graduated from university yet or did you take a gap year?'

'I didn't go to university.'

That surprised him too. University was a rite of passage in his circle whether the person was academic or not. 'What do you do?'

He waited for the stock answer of 'charity work'.

There was a momentary hesitation and her face flushed with colour. 'I'm in hospitality.'

He could have laughed. After charity work, hospitality was a great favourite for the idle rich wanting to make a point of their usefulness.

No wonder she blushed at the admission.

It surprised him, though. Tabitha struck him as being from a different mould to the usual socialites who filled his world.

What a waste of a good brain and a life, being content to spend days shopping and holidaying. It was a mindset he'd never understood. Giannis had been fortunate to be raised within one of Europe's wealthiest families and, like his sisters, had inherited thirty million euros on his twenty-first birthday, but it was not in the Basinas nature to be idle. Undoubtedly wealth was something to be enjoyed but it was also a tool to create more wealth, not just for him but for others.

Giannis's inheritance had been used to build a diverse portfolio of businesses which collectively employed over five thousand people. He had exacting standards, and demanded the best from every person he employed, no matter their position, but he rewarded them well for it both in pay and perks. The staff here in his palace hotel, for example, were considered the best paid hotel staff in the whole of Europe.

He did not understand how people could sleep if their wealth was generated by the unrewarded sweat of others.

He did not understand how people could actively seek to be freeloaders.

His wife had been a freeloader. She'd been many things. A liar. A gold-digger. A cheat. Even now, five years after the fact, five years since she and her unborn child had died, the anger and bitterness still lived, muted but still there.

He'd buried his wife and her child, and while the other mourners had mourned he'd had to bite his tongue to stop himself from ripping into their grief.

He would never allow himself to lose his anger entirely. If he forgot what it felt like he would lay himself open to making the same mistake again and Giannis never made the same mistake twice.

He'd been blinded by his wife's beautiful façade to the lies beneath it.

What lay beneath this woman's façade?

His fingers itched to pull the mask off Tabitha's face and see if it was as beautiful as he suspected.

Her own fingers lifted her champagne flute to her lips.

A tiny drop of gold liquid spilled out of the corner of her mouth. A pink tongue darted out to capture it.

Veins heating at the less than chaste images that tiny action produced, Giannis drank some more of his champagne and swallowed it slowly.

Theos, he could not remember when he'd last been so physically aware of a woman.

He could not remember ever being so captivated by one.

Whatever lay beneath her façade, he could enjoy their time together and enjoy the heady feelings that erupted through him to hold her in his arms.

He rose to his feet and held out a hand to her. 'Ready for another dance?'

Cornflower-blue eyes met his. A shy smile formed on her lips.

When her fingers wrapped around his he felt a shock of electricity dart through his skin.

Time slipped away from her.

Tabitha knew she was a fool for saying yes to another dance. She was a fool for not having made her excuses and left.

She could make all the excuses she wanted but the simple truth was she wanted to stay. She wanted this feeling to last as long as it could because she would never feel it again.

She would never have this night again.

Once the ball was over she would never dance with Giannis again.

Come the morning she would revert back to being a chambermaid and this night would be nothing but a memory.

She was in the midst of the most wonderful of dreams and she didn't want to wake up.

They danced. They drank more champagne. They danced again.

The hands that held as they danced clasped tightly, their forearms pressing together.

The hand that had rested just above the small of her back moved up so it palmed her bare skin. She had never imagined the thrills that could race through her veins at a mere touch of flesh upon flesh.

Their eyes stayed locked. The guests surrounding them were nothing but blocks of colour in the periphery of her vision.

When the next group dance started there were no words to communicate their unspoken agreement to leave the dance floor.

More champagne was consumed.

Time slipped even faster. She tried her hardest to hold on to it but the great clock on the wall ticked on.

As midnight approached the dances slowed in tempo but Tabitha felt giddy. The champagne she'd drunk, the setting, the arms holding her so closely, the undiminished attention from the clear blue eyes holding hers...

She felt as if she were coming to life. Never before had she been so aware of the blood pumping through her body, of the beats of her heart, of the sensitivity of her skin.

And never before had she been so aware of another. Giannis. The olive skin, the strong throat, the strong jaw, the rise and fall of his chest...the sensuous mouth.

She no longer cared that he had the power to make her homeless with nothing but a single word. Maybe it was the champagne doing her thinking for her but these were feelings she had never known before. Tomorrow was tomorrow. Right now it didn't exist.

'The fireworks start soon,' he murmured into her ear. 'Watch them with me.'

She shivered at the sensation of his breath against her skin. Her fingers reflexively tightened on his. They were pressed so tightly together her breasts were crushed through the fabric of her dress and his suit against his chest.

She smiled her answer.

His lips curved.

The orchestra was reaching the end of its piece.

Giannis put his nose to her ear and breathed in the soft, floral scent.

He ached to take this ravishing creature somewhere private and feel those heart-shaped lips against his own.

When he had imagined this night he had seen himself dancing with a parade of women, making bored small talk in the vain hope one might capture his attention.

He'd never imagined he would find someone before the dancing had even started and be greedy to keep her in his arms. Ballroom dancing was a chore he'd endured at his boarding school but there was nothing chore-like about dancing with this enigmatic woman with whom small talk had proven itself unnecessary. He could dance with her all night. He *would* dance with her all night.

But the dancing was about to finish for a short period while the orchestra took a break and the firework display took place.

He knew the best spot to watch it with her.

Drifting his hand further up her back, marvelling at the soft texture of her skin, he found the spot where her spine formed at the base of her neck and circled a finger around it. Then he pressed his cheek against hers, a last contact of their bodies before he pulled away and guided her out of the ballroom.

Hands clasped tightly together, they walked past the champagne fountain. He picked a glass up and handed it to her then took one for himself.

The corridor they stepped into was deserted but the rooms they passed were full of revellers wanting a break from the dancing for food or to rest their feet.

Outside in the gardens, the scent of roses in bloom filled the warm air.

Giannis loved the palace hotel gardens at night. Beautiful though it was by day, the night brought a new dimension to it, imagery from childhood books coming to life amongst the carved statues, water fountains and, further back, in the thick hedges that formed the famed maze.

The spot he took Tabitha to was in a white gazebo in a secluded part of the garden. She stared at the vast structure perfectly suited to such lavish grounds and imagined aristocracy from centuries ago treading this same path.

Flutes of champagne in hand, they stood at the balustrade, arms pressed together, and watched the guests spill out onto the vast lawn, but they were blurs in Tabitha's eyes, her senses too attuned to the man beside her for anything else to sink in with any substance.

'How long are you in Vienna for?' he asked casually, a question to make her stomach turn.

Before she could think of an answer, the moonlight caught one of the figures on the lawn, mask removed. Tabitha's blood turned cold in an instant as recognition flashed at her.

It was her stepsister, Fiona.

She hadn't had any communication with her in well over four years, not since Tabitha had been forced to leave the family home.

So many emotions rushed through her to see Fiona there, dressed in a beautiful gown that no doubt had been paid for by money intended to be Tabitha's inheritance, but the primary emotion that shot through her like an echo was fear.

Fiona had made her life a living hell.

Tabitha's fingers tightened around the now empty champagne flute, but she must have exerted too much subconscious pressure for the glass shattered in her hand.

She jumped back as shards of glass fell to the ground, too shocked at seeing her stepsister—how had she not noticed her before?—to realise her hand was bleeding until she caught Giannis's concerned stare.

He snatched at her hand and peered closely at it. 'Are you okay?'

She inhaled deeply through the shock and stinging pain and managed to nod.

'We should get a doctor to look at this. I'll make a call and see if we have one here.' Still holding her hand, he used his free hand to tug off the black cravat around his neck.

'I don't need a doctor.' A drop of blood rolled off the palm of her hand. She took another deep breath. 'It's superficial. Just a cut.'

She would have argued against a doctor even if she'd severed half her hand. The last thing she wanted was to draw attention to herself. The mask and the dress gave her anonymity amongst her colleagues but if anyone who knew her were to look too closely the game would be over. Now she knew Fiona was here—and maybe Saffron too—she dared not risk it. It wasn't just that her identity would be blown. The thought of seeing either of them without any preparation was an ordeal she was in no way ready to put herself through.

She remembered the day she'd first met them and how excited she'd been at the thought of having two big sisters, along with a new mother, and her heart clenched at the trusting innocence of her ten-year-old self.

The cravat freed, Giannis gave it a sharp flick then wrapped it gently around her bleeding hand. 'That's a lot of blood for a superficial cut.'

'That's the body doing what it's designed to do. I'll find a bathroom and clean it out.'

He kept his hand on the cravat wrapped around her cut. 'My apartment is right behind us. We can clean it there and assess for damage.'

She was quite sure the flow of blood seeping from her wound increased at the casual way he said 'we'.

When her gaze drifted back up to meet his eyes there was a lurch in both her heart and stomach.

If the choice was to dart across the garden and risk facing her stepsister, or to go to the apartment of this man who, despite his being a virtual stranger, she felt a strange sense of safety being with...

CHAPTER THREE

TABITHA DIDN'T THINK of the foolhardiness of going to Giannis's one-storey apartment until he closed the front door behind them and even then it was more of a dim chiding in the back of her head. And it wasn't about the foolishness of being alone with a man she hardly knew while fireworks exploded in the sky around them.

It was the foolishness of her own feelings.

Her every action that night had been foolhardy from the moment she had accepted Mrs Coulter's wonderful generosity.

She held Giannis's cravat tightly against her stinging wounded hand and tried to take in her surroundings.

Tabitha knew he'd converted the old staff quarters into a base for himself for the few days a month he was there—she currently lived in the new staff quarters—but none of the staff had been invited in before.

But as she followed Giannis down a wide hallway the huge living room they passed barely registered, her attention completely taken with the man before her.

He pushed open a door to the right and stepped over the threshold.

She did the same and came to an immediate stop.

This was Giannis's bedroom.

He stopped walking and turned to face her. His features taut, his voice serious, he said, 'The light in my bathroom is the best to see with but if you don't feel comfortable coming in here we can clean the cut in the kitchen.'

How many foolish actions could a woman make in one evening?

She walked into the bedroom.

Her legs feeling as if they were walking on a cloud, she followed him past the largest bed she had ever seen in her life, vaguely noting the impersonal nature of the space and its lack of pictures or photos, her heart hammering, breaths shortening.

Tabitha had never been in a man's bedroom before.

Trying desperately to affect nonchalance, but knowing she was failing, she followed him through another door into a bathroom that was as luxurious as the bedroom was sparse.

Heart in her throat, she went straight to the double sink. From the corner of her eye she saw Giannis open a tall cupboard door and pull out what looked like a black leather washbag.

Carefully unwinding the cravat from her hand, she placed it in the right-hand sink then turned the left sink's tap on.

The bleeding had definitely lessened in flow.

'Your cravat is ruined,' she said in what she wanted to be a conversational tone but which sounded shaky even to her own ears. The cravat might be black but it was made of silk.

'It doesn't matter.' He placed the washbag beside the sink just as she put her hand under the running tap.

She clenched her teeth as the cold water hit.

'It hurts?' he asked.

'Only a bit,' she lied, feeling foolish to admit that a cut so minor smarted so much. There was soap in a dispenser above the sink and she squirted some onto the cut and rubbed it in, then held it back under the tap to let it clean out properly, all the while intensely aware that Giannis stood close enough that she could feel the heat emanating from him.

They had danced together for hours, their bodies almost flush, but her awareness of him had not been as heightened as it was now.

Every cell in her body had come to life and strained towards him.

'May I have a towel, please?' she asked when done.

'Let me,' he murmured, taking her injured hand back into his own.

Tabitha held her breath, suddenly aware of her heart hammering so hard its beats were thudding in her throat.

He'd removed his mask. The features she found so captivating were right there before her, the closest they had ever been, unadorned.

Head bowed in concentration, a lock of his dark brown hair fell over his eye. He dislodged it with a quick flick of his head. 'You can move your hand without problem?'

She cleared her throat and whispered, 'Yes.'

His movements unhurried, he wrapped a small grey hand-towel around her hand and gently pressed it to her palm.

Palm dry, he removed the towel. Fresh drop-

lets of blood seeped from the cut, although no-
ticeably less heavy than before. 'I should have a
bandage for that.' He placed the towel back on
the palm, took Tabitha's other hand and pressed
it on it. 'Keep the pressure on.'

He unzipped what she'd assumed to be a washbag but was in fact stuffed with bandages and
other first-aid equipment.

'Are you a secret doctor?' she asked, again
striving for lightness of tone and failing dismally.
His spicy scent was filling her senses again and
she struggled to even open her vocal cords.

Clear blue eyes briefly met hers, creasing at
the corners, before he pulled out a large pad-
ded plaster in a protective packet. 'A habit from
my university days. My mother insisted I take a
medical kit with me.'

Using his teeth, he ripped the packaging, the
tendons on his olive throat straining.

The blood running through her heated a little
more and she had to fight the fog in her brain
to think of something to say. 'Was your mother
over-protective?'

He gave a grunt-like laugh. 'She was sensible.
I was rather wild and reckless in my younger

years. Hold your hand flat but curve your fingers a little for me.'

She complied then held her breath again as he carefully fixed the plaster to her hand, smoothing it down at the sides.

'There,' he said, lifting her hand to his mouth and placing a kiss to the plaster. 'All done.'

Her belly flipped over so hard the effect rippled through the rest of her. 'Thank you.' But her vocal cords had now knotted themselves so tightly the words hardly formed.

He was so close. The cells in her body were no longer merely straining towards him; they were trying to fly out of her skin to him, abetted by the violent beats of her heart.

Giannis studied the delicate palm spread out on his hand and traced his fingers over her elegant ones, surprised to find the tips hardened and calloused.

About to ask how this could be, he met her cornflower-blue gaze and his throat closed up.

He'd tended to Tabitha's wounded hand with the best of intentions, promising himself they would clean it up and bandage it then go back outside to watch the fireworks together.

He hadn't considered that his attraction to her

would burn even brighter when they were alone in the confines of his apartment or that he would be so aware of her every movement and every breath.

He hadn't considered that he would tend to her hand and have to stop himself from running his tongue over it.

Since Anastasia's death he had hardly lived like a monk. He'd been with a considerable number of women, both before his marriage and after he was widowed.

Not one of them had made his loins ache and his chest tighten with one shy smile.

Not one of them had captivated him like Tabitha had, and he still hadn't seen her face...

Suddenly he found himself needing to see it, to see the whole face of this woman who had enchanted him so much that he couldn't determine if it was her or the champagne he'd drunk inducing it.

He released his hold on her hand and brought his fingers to her face.

Not a breath of sound could be heard between them as he slowly lifted the mask up and over the honey-blonde hair.

Heart pounding, he stared at a flawless face far more beautiful than he had suspected.

Truly, ethereally beautiful.

He rubbed the back of his fingers down high, rounded cheekbones in wonder, that wonder growing at the sudden pulse he saw in the cornflower eyes.

She gave a sharp inhalation before her own hand reached for his face and tentatively touched his jaw.

A bolt of electricity charged through him, strong enough to knock a weaker man off his feet.

The light delicacy of her floral perfume whirled into his senses.

Everything about this woman was delicate and faultless. Were it not for the warmth of her soft skin and the slight trembles he saw vibrating through her, he could have believed she was made from porcelain.

He traced his fingers across her oval jawline then dragged them down the elegant neck, lingering at the pulse throbbing at the spot before he reached her collarbone and took the one step needed to do what he had spent the entire evening hungering to do.

He brought his face down and captured her heart-shaped lips in his.

Another bolt of electricity rocketed through him, far stronger than the first, crashing hot through his veins and skin with a buzz that must have seeped through him, for Tabitha jolted too.

Pulling back slightly so their lips were barely touching, he opened his eyes and found hers fixed on him, a dazed expression shining at him. The fingers resting on his jaw had frozen.

The walls around him began to spin, heat flowing through him so fast and so thick he wondered if he *had* drunk more than he'd thought.

He found he didn't care.

Champagne, desire or a combination of both, at that moment he wanted this woman more than he had ever wanted anyone or anything.

Sliding an arm around her waist, he pulled her to him and moulded his mouth to hers, exploring the plump softness of her lips, then parting them to dart his tongue inside and explore the hot champagne-scented depths.

Tabitha succumbed to her very first kiss feeling like she'd fallen into a dream.

The whole night had been a dream.

But this…

It was mesmerising.

She met the strokes of his tongue tentatively at first but the heat bubbling inside her being fed by his heavenly kisses grew at a ferocious pace and smothered any inhibitions she should have had.

Grabbing at the soft leather of his swallowtail jacket to keep her suddenly boneless legs upright, she arched into the hard contours of his body and moved the hand clutched at his cheek to hook tightly around his neck.

She felt intoxicated, could feel the blood pumping in the veins of her mouth and moving relentlessly through the rest of her, heating wherever his firm hands swept over her.

She only realised he'd unpinned her hair when it spilled down over them.

He broke the kiss to turn his face into her hair and breathed it in deeply before bringing both hands to her face and smoothing the hair back.

His eyes had darkened, his hunger for her so stark that her stomach contracted.

Never had she imagined that this man would look at her with such desire in his eyes.

Before this night she hadn't imagined Giannis would *ever* look at her.

When his mouth found hers again, the kiss

harder and hungrier, fresh heat assailed her, threading through the very fabric of her being, and she tightened her hold around him, suddenly aching for him to rip the beautiful but constricting dress from her burning, sensitised skin.

As if his mind was aligned with her own, Giannis lifted her effortlessly into his arms, the motion making her belly swoop.

The world's biggest rollercoaster could not have had a greater effect. Or felt a fraction as heady.

The feelings rippling through her were like nothing she had even suspected could exist. Her world—her *universe*—had shrunk so it contained only Giannis.

He carried her to the bedroom and set her down gently on her feet beside the bed.

During that short walk he'd turned the bedroom light off so they were illuminated only by the light pouring in from his bathroom and the fireworks lighting the sky outside.

His throat moved as his hooded eyes stared at her so hard, she felt stripped naked beneath it.

'*Eisai omorfi,*' he breathed as he tugged her to him again.

She didn't have a clue what he'd said but pleasure soaked through her at the way he'd spoken the words.

Their arms wrapped around each other and she sank into another invasion of his hungry tongue assaulting her in the most heavenly way.

Reckless, intoxicating madness had caught Giannis in its grip. He *knew* this was madness: making love to a woman he knew only by first name. Tabitha could have stepped out of one of the fairy-tale books his sisters had read as children, an enchantress casting her spell over him.

If this was a spell, he did not want to find the cure to it. Not yet. He wanted to stay under her enchantment and let it take him wherever it desired.

He dragged his mouth down the column of her throat to where the pulse at the base of her neck now raged while her fingers snaked into his hair and dug into his scalp.

Too many clothes, he thought dimly, his fingers working furiously at the back of her dress, trying to find the hidden buttons. His thumb ran over the bump of a small clasp. He popped it open and immediately found the hidden zip.

In one fluid motion he pulled it down to the base of her spine.

He ran his hands flat over the length of her back and sucked in a breath when he found no bra.

He brought his mouth back to claim her in another hot, hard kiss and shrugged his jacket off, then stepped back, giving himself just enough room to undo the top three buttons of his shirt, then tugged it up and over his face. He threw it to the floor.

Breathing deeply, he gazed again at the captivating face in front of him before closing the small distance he'd just created to place his hands on her shoulders.

His fingers drifted over the soft skin to the band of her dress, which was defying gravity and staying up.

All it needed was one small tug at the waist to help it on its way.

It fell with a whoosh to her feet.

His throat closed as he drank in the body now naked bar a pair of skimpy white knickers.

Thee mou.

Upturned breasts, plumper than the dress had allowed his mind to imagine, a slim waist and rounded hips...

She was all woman.

She was exquisite.

Unthinkingly, he cupped one of the breasts and ran a thumb over the erect tip.

She swayed. Her lips parted and a small gasp escaped from her.

He gripped her tightly at the hips and lowered himself down to capture the breast his hand cupped with his mouth.

Blood pooled hot and hard in his groin, making his rock-hard arousal throb tightly against the constriction of his leather trousers.

She tasted…incredible.

She swayed again, legs visibly trembling, the fingers on his head digging in harder.

Rising, he shuffled her back until the back of her legs touched the bed.

Chest rising and falling rapidly, hands still reaching for him, she sat.

His arousal had become too painful to endure a moment longer and, not tearing his eyes from hers, he quickly undid his trousers and pushed them down his hips.

Tabitha gazed at the first erection she had ever seen in the flesh and her pelvis contracted all over again.

Her mouth full of moisture, heart thumping painfully, her gaze drifted over the rest of him.

Giannis was beautiful.

His tall frame was broader and far more muscular than she'd imagined—and she *had* imagined it, in many unbidden moments when the only thing she'd needed to use her brain for was changing bed sheets. Only a small line of hair covered his chest, starting from just above his abdomen, but thickened and darkened considerably at the area where his huge length jutted out proudly.

She felt too intoxicated with all the heat swirling like a furnace inside her to be scared.

Never in her life had she craved something as much as she craved Giannis in this moment. There was something about him that sang to her on a fundamental level she had no chance of understanding so she did the only thing she could do and embraced it.

When he'd divested himself of the rest of his clothing and joined her on the bed, pushing her down so she was flat on her back, she opened her arms to him.

His lips found hers in another crushing kiss

and then he was exploring her, using his hands and mouth to cover her body, setting fire to her skin, melting her bones.

He lavished attention on breasts she had never suspected could be so sensitive and yet so receptive. He kissed her belly button, he kissed her sides…and then he tugged her knickers down and kissed her right in the core of her womanhood.

At the first touch of his tongue on her swollen nub she jerked wildly, sensation shooting through her.

Dear God…

One hand grasped his head, the other reaching up to grab a pillow.

Pleasure pooled thick and heavy deep within her and she instinctively lifted her bottom; instinctive, as the action came not from her brain.

Her brain had ceased to function on anything but a primitive level.

Her *body* had ceased to function on anything but a primitive level.

The only coherent thought in her head was Giannis's name playing like a distant echo.

Only when he'd snaked his way back up her

body, sheathed himself deftly and his mouth hovered over hers for another kiss, his hips lodged between her parted legs, his arousal hard at the top of her thigh, did she get the coherence to gasp, 'Please be gentle.'

The lips that had been about to claim hers reared back, a question forming in the crease of his brow.

Suddenly afraid that the truth would put an abrupt end to this most magical of moments, she hooked an arm around his neck and pulled him down to mould her mouth to his.

He kissed her back hungrily and shifted his hips so his erection was right where it needed to be.

And then he slid inside her damp heat. Slowly, deliberately slowly, stretching her, giving her the time to adjust and accommodate…

Her eyes flew open as a sharp pain seared through her, fleeting then dissolving…

And then *she* dissolved.

Her bones softened, her hips arched, she scraped her fingers into his head and parted her lips as he drove into her, the pleasure so intense that all she could do was cling to him and let him move inside her with long strokes, every thrust increasing the sensation, every groan from his lips against her ear feeding it.

He filled her completely. Perfectly.

A large hand skimmed roughly down her side and reached under her bottom, lifting her so their groins ground together, heightening the pleasure to a level that turned her into a mass of nerve endings.

Faster and harder he thrust into her, and faster and harder her hips bucked back, and all the while the sensation that had started life deep inside her spread until, without any warning, pleasure ripped through her, so intense that colour brighter and more explosive than any firework filled her.

It must have been enough to tip Giannis over the edge too for the fingers still holding her bottom clamped tightly on her flesh and his huge body tensed then shuddered.

Long moments later, he collapsed on top of her, breathing heavily in her ear.

It took a long while for Tabitha's world to right itself and for her heart to regain something that resembled a normal rhythm.

A delicious lethargy came over her. Her eyes closed and the world drifted away.

* * *

The sound of a door closing woke Tabitha with a start.

She sat bolt upright, horrified to find dusky light pouring through the bedroom window.

She looked at her watch and saw the time was six a.m.

No, no, *no*.

She was due to start work in an hour.

She strained her ears and heard the sound of a coffee machine working.

Giannis must be in the kitchen.

How long did she have to escape?

She cursed herself and tried her hardest to breathe but panic had set in.

Clutching her fuzzy head, she darted her gaze around the room, looking for her dress.

It was draped on the arm chair in the corner. Giannis must have put it there.

She swallowed back a surge of nausea and cursed herself again.

Stupid, idiotic, fool!

Bad enough she'd got so carried away with the romance of the evening and the undeniable yet fatal attraction that had sparked to life between her and Giannis to sleep with him in the first place, but to stay the whole night?

What complete and utter stupidity.

Her cheeks burned as she recalled them making love a second time…

She staggered off the bed and instinctively covered her nakedness.

She had never slept naked in her life!

Snatching the dress, she found his own masquerade costume beneath it, his black shirt at the top.

She debated for a nanosecond before pulling the shirt he hadn't fully unbuttoned over her head and hurriedly pulled her knickers on, all the while thinking of the best way to escape, wishing she had paid more attention to the layout of the apartment when she'd had the chance.

But of course, she hadn't paid attention. She'd been too drunk on the strange alchemy of Giannis and champagne to pay attention to *anything*.

Quickly she scanned her surroundings from the window. The grounds were empty of life but they wouldn't be for long. Any minute an army of workers would be out there to clear up any mess revellers had made during the event.

She opened the window, threw her dress and shoes out of it, then squeezed herself out behind them.

Bare feet on the cold ground, she scooped her belongings into her arms and fled.

Giannis whistled as he poured the freshly brewed coffee into glass cups, placed them on a tray with milk and sugar and continued whistling as he made his way back to his bedroom where he'd left his enchantress sleeping.

He could not remember the last time he'd awoken in such a good mood. Years.

Could Tabitha be the one his sisters had been nagging him to find? He knew next to nothing about her but if she could afford a ticket to his ball, and that dress which must have cost more than the ticket, she obviously had wealth. She'd been educated at one of the UK's finest boarding schools. And they had a chemistry that was off the scale.

He'd never known a night like it.

Whether Tabitha was the future Mrs Basinas or not, right then his intention was to bring her coffee and climb back into bed with her. He hoped she hadn't made any plans. He'd already messaged his PA to inform her he wouldn't be returning to Santorini that day and to rearrange his appointments.

Still whistling, he carried the tray to his bedroom and opened the door...

The bed was empty.

'Tabitha?' he called. She must be in the bathroom...

The bathroom door was open.

He placed the tray on his dresser and, as he did so, he noticed something else that had gone. Her ball gown.

Two minutes later, every room in the apartment searched, he returned to his bedroom perplexed and angry.

She had run out on him.

From the corner of his eye, something sparkly caught his eye.

He strode to the bed where the sparkly item was and found, on the pillow on which her exquisite head had rested, one of her earrings.

CHAPTER FOUR

'THE FILE IS INCOMPLETE.' Giannis tapped his long fingers on the thick file which allegedly contained the details and photograph of every guest who'd attended the masquerade ball two weeks ago, when he'd learned there had been no guest by the name of Tabitha on the list. He'd spent the morning studying the dossiers so thoroughly he was quite sure he could bump into any of the guests in this file and relate their name, age and occupation without introduction.

But the one face he'd wanted to find was missing.

His PA sighed. 'That is the entire list of attendees. It has been triple checked.'

'Then someone must have gate-crashed the ball.'

At this, Giannis's head of security spoke up. 'Every guest was checked off on the system.'

'Then the system must have been faulty or someone forged an invitation.' He hadn't explained why he thought this. Giannis hadn't explained himself to anyone for years. Unless you counted his sisters, who pried into his life with a thoroughness that would make a Russian spy envious.

'Every invitation was inspected and the names ticked off electronically. The only way it could have been done was for someone to steal an invitation but there were no reported thefts. Everyone who should have been there was there and accounted for. There was only one no-show: an elderly Swiss gentleman who was hospitalised after a fall that day.'

Giannis drummed his fingers with more force against the file, thinking hard.

Tabitha had vanished without a trace. Were it not for the earring left on his pillow and his missing shirt—had she taken it?—he could have believed he'd been under a real enchantment and imagined the whole encounter.

He'd had unplanned one-night stands before but never had he had a woman run out on him as Tabitha had done.

That was if she was even called Tabitha.

Somehow, a woman had foiled the ball's tight

security. She had made a fool of his security system and made a fool of him.

It brought a rancid taste to his tongue to imagine how she must be laughing at him.

He would have let the whole thing go, put it down to experience and forgotten all about her... were it not for the strong suspicion that she'd been a virgin.

Pushing his chair back, Giannis got to his feet. 'I'm going to take a swim. Josie, call my flight crew. Tell them we'll be returning to Santorini in two hours.'

Leaving his PA to make the arrangements, he left his office and strolled through the lobby of his hotel.

What a waste of a valuable day. He could have read the thick dossier of guests from the comfort of his home, should have distrusted his gut which had nagged him that being here at his Viennese palace hotel would bring him closer to Tabitha.

Now he intended to do what he should have done the moment he'd found her gone—forget about her.

Striding down the long, wide corridor that led to the hotel's luxury leisure facilities, he saw in the distance a couple of chambermaids talking, their heads bowed over something.

When he was three doors from them, the chambermaids separated, one entering the room to the left, the other the room to the right. By the time he passed they were wheeling their trolleys loaded with fresh bedding and cleaning products in behind them.

There was something about the blonde one...

Unbidden, his feet ground to a halt and he turned around, only to catch a glimpse of a swishing blonde ponytail before the suite's door closed behind her.

His heart suddenly pounding, Giannis stared at the shut door for a long moment before he blinked some sense into himself and carried on his way.

He had to accept that the woman he'd shared the most miraculous night of his life with was some form of confidence trickster and the chances of him ever finding her were slim.

It was time to forget about her.

Tabitha, her back resting against the door of the suite she'd just entered, held her trembling hand to her beating chest, hardly daring to breathe.

Had he seen her?

Worse, had he recognised her?

Legs shaking, she slid down the door until her bottom reached the floor and dragged long gulps of air into her lungs.

When she'd been told by a panicking colleague that the big boss had unexpectedly turned up she'd been grateful to have her trolley to hold on to. It had stopped her visibly swaying. She'd felt the blood pooling from her head down to her feet.

The two weeks since the ball had been awful, her feelings alternating between guilt at running away from Giannis and terror that he would discover who she really was. A lowly worker. Not the rich woman he'd assumed and which she'd let him believe. Every time there was a knock on her bedroom door in the staff quarters fear would grip her that her identity had been discovered. Visions of being unceremoniously escorted from the palace hotel plagued her.

Guilt consumed her too. Recalling how she'd been swept away by the romance of the ball, by the attraction that had blazed between them, by the consumption of all that champagne, didn't change a thing.

The champagne had lowered her inhibitions but it hadn't acted for her.

She should have left the ball and returned to her quarters the moment Giannis had showed an interest in her.

But if she had then she would never have shared such a wonderful night with him.

She hugged her knees, wishing she could run after him, explain herself and apologise but there was no way she could do that and keep her job. He would be rightly disgusted with her.

She was disgusted with herself, a disgust that had grown ever since she'd used the staff computer to seek pictures of him. All she'd wanted was to see his face again but all she'd done was unleash a whirl of new emotions within herself. The first pictures that came up in the search were of Giannis and his dead wife. There had been many pictures of the happy couple together.

Tabitha had stayed glued to that computer for so long, her eyes had become gritty.

Anastasia Basinas had been the sexiest, most beautiful woman Tabitha had ever seen, a stunner with thick, glossy raven hair and a knowing gleam in her cat-like eyes. There had been a particular picture of the two of them together on their lavishly celebrated wedding day. Giannis had looked at his new bride with what could only be described as devotion.

They had clearly been madly in love.

Anastasia's death, which she read had occurred in a car crash five years ago, must have devastated him.

The mild nausea that had been swirling in her belly since she'd taken her break intensified and she forced herself back to her feet and propelled herself to the bathroom, where she heaved the contents of her lunch up.

'You're looking very peaky, dear. Are you not feeling well? You're not still worrying about the earring are you? I did tell you not to.'

Tabitha managed a smile and shook her head. She *did* still feel guilty about the lost earring but that wasn't the reason she looked peaky.

Mrs Coulter gave a stern stare. 'Then eat something. You're going to waste away.'

To stop the elderly woman worrying, Tabitha took a small bite from a cheese and cucumber sandwich.

'That's better. What time do you finish today?'

'Midnight. I've got four hours off from three.'

'You should use that time to rest. You look exhausted.'

Tabitha swallowed the small morsel and prayed her stomach would keep it down until she'd left Mrs Coulter's suite.

It had been the same thing now for two whole weeks. Every day at around the same time, she became nauseous. What she'd initially thought was shock at Giannis's unexpected appearance at the hotel had become a daily occurrence. As had the strange exhaustion that cloaked her, which Mrs Coulter had picked up on.

And then had come the realisation that her period was five days late.

She'd taken the test three days ago. Then she'd taken another.

For three days she'd felt as if she were living in purgatory. She was sure Mrs Coulter would give her a sympathetic ear but she'd resisted confiding in her.

The first person she needed to tell was Giannis. And that was who she was going to see as soon as her shift was finished.

He'd flown into Vienna that morning and, as far as Tabitha was aware, was staying for one night only.

It was too late to worry about her job. Too late to worry that she could hit rock bottom again.

She'd already hit it.

The knock on Giannis's office door interrupted his perusal of the palace hotel accounts. When he was satisfied that everything was in order, he would read through the guest book for feedback from the people who really mattered. The paying guests.

'Come in,' he called.

Josie, his PA who travelled everywhere with him, entered the office, a crease on her usually unflappable brow. 'I have a young lady here to see you. I've told her you're not to be disturbed but she won't take no for an answer.'

'I'm too busy,' he dismissed. Once he'd finished his monthly appraisal of the books and guest satisfaction he had his monthly meeting with the hotel senior management team to chair, followed by a dinner date with his sister, who'd turned up at his villa that morning announcing she was coming to Vienna with him.

'She says to tell you her name is Tabitha.'

His heart inflated like a hot air balloon, punching the air from his lungs, and he had to grind his feet to the carpeted floor beneath him to stop himself jumping out of his chair.

She was here?

Tamping down the eruption that had exploded inside him, Giannis nodded curtly. 'Give me two minutes then let her in.'

Josie, betraying no surprise, nodded and slipped back out of the office.

Once the door was closed, Giannis rested back in his chair and sucked a lungful of air back in.

His throat had run dry.

He poured himself a glass of water and drank it in three swallows.

Once he'd regained a little of his equilibrium, he bent his head over the accounts spread out on his desk, dragging more air into his lungs, trying to establish regular breathing.

By the time the next knock on his door echoed, he was prepared.

'Come in.'

The door opened.

A petite figure appeared, dressed all in black, blonde hair tied back.

His heart slammed against his ribs.

She pushed the door shut behind her.

Cornflower-blue eyes met his.

His heart slammed again.

Not a word was exchanged between them.

Blood whooshed in his head as Giannis stared at the face that had haunted him this past month.

His efforts to forget her had been spectacularly unsuccessful.

This was the woman he had shared the most incredible night of his life with, the woman who had then run away and stayed away...until now.

She was much paler than he remembered. More fragile looking. But, even in ordinary clothing, every bit as beautiful.

Slowly he let his eyes drift over her and as he did so he noticed other details.

Like that the ordinary clothing she wore was the black trousers and black polo shirt with his hotel's motif embroidered on the left side of the chest that all his hotel's cleaning staff wore.

He flattened his hands on the desk and leaned forward, hardly able to believe what his eyes were telling him. 'You work for me?'

Hands wringing together, she pulled her lips in and nodded.

Incredulous, he swept his eyes again over the anonymous uniform designed to make the predominantly female staff who cleaned his hotel's rooms and suites feel safe. 'How long?'

She closed her eyes. 'I'm sorry.'

'How long?' he repeated icily. The shock and elation that had suckered him at the first mention of her name was steadily morphing into anger.

He had spent weeks searching for this woman. He'd thrown numerous resources at the futile attempt to locate her and then, when he'd made the choice to abandon his search, had still found her lodged in his thoughts. She'd become an earworm he could not rid himself of.

The throat he had run his tongue down moved. 'Six months.'

Six months?

She'd been in his employ and under his nose all along?

His anger ratcheted up a notch.

'How the hell did you get a ticket for the ball?' he asked in the same icy tone. 'Did you steal it?'

'I was given it.'

'Someone gave you a forty-thousand euro ticket?' he mocked. 'What extra services did you have to do to receive that?'

Colour slashed the rounded cheekbones. 'Nothing like you're thinking.'

'And how do you know what I'm thinking, Tabitha…is that your real name? Or something else you lied about?'

'It's my real name,' she whispered then, hands still wringing together, paced to the small sofa in the corner of his office.

'I did not invite you to sit down,' he snapped.

Slim shoulders rose in a shrug and she sat regardless and hunched forward, forearms resting on her thighs. 'I'm sorry for lying. I was given the ticket and the dress.'

'By who?'

'It doesn't matter.' Tabitha was struggling to breathe. She'd entered Giannis's office full of resolve and determination but then she'd found herself engulfed by his spicy scent and everything inside her had cramped and tightened, all except for her heart, which thundered hard beneath her ribs.

She had dreaded this moment. She had longed for it too. Longed to see him again.

How could you miss someone when you'd shared only one night with them? One night out of over the eight thousand she had spent on this earth but it had altered her place on this earth.

The most wonderful night of her life. With the most unimaginable consequences.

She could feel the antipathy radiating from him. She couldn't blame him for it. She deserved it. Her behaviour, especially when she had run out on him without a word of goodbye, had been unforgiveable.

If she could live that night again she would do everything differently but wishing for the past to rewrite itself didn't change the facts of today.

She'd expected to be met with anger but she couldn't deny the faint hope that had lived inside her that he would be happy to see her.

The clear blue eyes that had stared into hers with such hunger were icy cold as he leaned forward. 'I want to know who gave a chambermaid of my hotel a ticket for my ball when the guest list was by strict invitation only.'

She clamped her lips together. The darkness emanating from him made her think she would be better off protecting Mrs Coulter from this. Her wonderful friend didn't deserve to have Giannis's ire turned on her.

Tabitha had shared one magical night with this man but she didn't know him. From his reputation, she knew he had a ruthless streak. She would not risk turning that ruthlessness onto an elderly woman who'd wanted only for Tabitha to have one night of fun.

His eyes narrowed at her silence. 'Then you leave me no choice. Hotel staff were warned the ball was for paying guests only and that any attempt to infiltrate it would lead to the termination of their employment. On that basis, you're fired.'

'I'm pregnant.'

The words blurted from her tongue before she could stop them. They'd been hovering there since she'd walked into the office, waiting for the right time to be uttered.

But there had been no right time. What right time could there be for two virtual strangers to learn they were going to have a baby?

Never had she seen the colour drain from someone's face so quickly.

Clear blue eyes ringing with shock stared at her. 'What?'

'I'm pregnant.'

'Pregnant?'

She nodded and finally expelled the breath she'd been holding.

'Who's the father?'

Those three words landed like individual slaps to her face but she didn't drop her gaze. 'You are.'

He stared at her for the longest time and then, to her utter astonishment, Giannis threw his head back and laughed. The maniacal quality to it made her want to cover her ears.

'Please, don't,' she beseeched.

Still laughing, he pushed his chair back and got to his feet. Striding to the door, he opened it. 'Your time is up. I will let Giselle know your contract is to be terminated with immediate effect. Either you leave voluntarily or I call security and have you escorted out.'

'Giannis, please.'

The humour vanished. 'If any of what you say is true then a DNA test will prove it once the so-called baby is born. Until that time, your benefactor can deal with it. Now, get out before I throw you out.'

'You don't believe me, do you?' she whispered, hugging her arms across her chest to stave off the chill that had enveloped her.

'*Believe* you?' Without any warning, he slammed the door he'd been holding open for her shut, making her jump with the force of it.

When he looked at her there was nothing but contempt to be found in his stare. 'You let me believe you were a real guest and a woman of wealth.' Anger thickened his accent. 'You shared my bed then ran out on me and now you expect me to believe you're pregnant even though we used contraception?'

'We didn't the second time.'

The memory of reaching for her in his sleep suddenly flashed in Giannis's mind and his blood chilled.

He hadn't used a condom to begin with. He'd groped in the dark for one when he'd already been deep inside her.

The memory alone was enough to heat the sudden chill and thicken his loins.

It didn't matter that she was a liar of extraordinary talent, better even than Anastasia, who could have won a gold medal for deceit. His awareness for Tabitha had not abated in the slightest.

He remembered when he'd discovered that Anastasia had been playing him for a fool. Every lick of desire for her had been extinguished in that instant.

Tabitha was every bit as bad as his wife had

been but the ache to haul her into his arms and taste those delectable lips anew thrummed inside him.

Never in a thousand years would he have believed her to be anything but a woman of breeding and wealth. She must have practised that cut-glass accent. The nerve it must have taken to tell the barefaced lie that she'd attended Beddingdales, one of the most exclusive all-girls boarding schools in Europe... She hadn't skipped a beat. It had been a prepared lie, just as everything else had been.

'Who is the puppet master behind your honey trap?' he demanded to know.

Her face paled again, cornflower eyes widening, pretty brow creasing. 'What...? There was no honey trap. You approached me first.'

'Do you expect me to believe it was coincidence you were walking down the stairs at the exact moment I entered the hotel from my apartment? It would have been easy to watch me walk from my apartment from a window on the first or second floor and time your appearance to match mine.'

A flash of anger sparked from her eyes. 'That's absurd.'

'Is it? Someone bought you, a chambermaid, a ticket and outfit to wear for the ball. What was the reason behind it if not to seduce me and entrap me?'

'I didn't seduce you!' she cried. 'Don't rewrite what happened between us just because you don't like the idea that you slept with the hired help. What happened between us just… happened.'

'I could understand if someone had paid for your ticket to accompany them but you attended the ball alone. Why was that? Why did your benefactor not attend with you?'

'They couldn't.'

'Why not?'

'Because…' Her shoulders hunched as she obviously thought of the most convenient lie to tell. 'They just couldn't. But, I promise you, there was no ulterior motive. They just wanted to do something nice for me.'

'A very expensive way of doing something nice,' he mocked. 'Who was it? A rich family member?' That would be the only answer he would find vaguely acceptable, although that would then beg the question of who would allow a member of their family to work in a job that involved cleaning other people's messes if they had the kind of wealth at their disposal to purchase a forty-thousand euro ticket for a masquerade ball.

She took a deep breath and shook her head.

'Who is your benefactor?'

'It isn't important.'

'I disagree. No one would spend that amount of money on someone without expecting something in return. I want to know who your benefactor is and what you had to do in lieu of payment for attending a ball which you were expressly forbidden from attending.'

'I don't know what circles you mix in but you should look at expanding it.' There was a tremor in her voice. 'There are good people in the world and my benefactor is one of them. There was no ulterior motive. I know I let you believe I was a wealthy woman, and I'm sorry for that, but I didn't have a choice—if I'd confessed who I was you would have fired me on the spot.'

'You can try and talk your way out of it but the facts are indisputable. You posed as a paying guest. You spent the evening in my arms on the dance floor and in my bed. Strange behaviour for a woman who now claims she couldn't tell me her true identity for fear of losing her job. If you were so concerned with keeping it, you wouldn't have attempted this charade in the first place. You certainly wouldn't have gone to bed with me.'

Even though her gaze was now on his carpeted floor, he could see the stain of colour on her cheeks.

It was the same colour that had flushed on her cheeks when she'd come with him buried deep inside her.

Theos, every cell in his body ached to feel that sensation again, of being so deep inside her they could have been fused together.

This woman could confess to being a mass murderer and he would still want her.

But she wasn't confessing to anything and made no attempt to defend herself.

'Your denials are pitiful,' he said coldly, hating her but hating himself more for still wanting her. 'You set out to entrap me and, if your claim that you're pregnant proves to be true, then you have hit the jackpot.'

She lifted her head to look him square in the eye. 'How?' she challenged. 'Tell me, please, how an unplanned pregnancy can be described as hitting the jackpot?'

'If you really are pregnant and the child proves to be mine, you have a meal ticket for life.'

'If?' She jumped to her feet. 'I *am* pregnant and you *are* the father. Go and buy me a pregnancy test if you don't believe me! There hasn't been anyone else. And I don't want a meal ticket. All I want is some financial support...'

Fury thumped violently through him. He strode over to her and stared at the angry, beautiful face, his heart pumping harder as that delicate scent swirled into his senses.

One night he had spent with this deceitful woman and her scent had imprinted itself on him.

He had never despised anyone as much as he despised her at that moment.

'I knew there would be a financial aspect in all this. There always is with women like you.'

'Women like me?' Her outrage vibrated from her very pores then her face contorted, her hands flew forward and she shoved his chest. 'Are you implying that I'm a whore because I slept with you?' she shouted. 'What does that make you? A gigolo?'

He grabbed her wrists before she could push him again. 'I did not call you a whore!'

'You implied it!'

'I did not. That must be your conscience.'

'I was a *virgin*.'

CHAPTER FIVE

TABITHA WAS SO fired up with anger and shame, her awareness of him fizzing over her skin and buzzing through her veins, that if he hadn't had such a tight hold of her wrists she would have slapped him.

Suddenly she found herself against the office wall, his hands either side of her face.

His features were taut as he stared at her, his long nose inches from hers, clear blue eyes pulsing with fury but also with something she recognised from their night together...

Her heart thrashed so wildly he must have been able to feel the beats against his chest which brushed against her breasts.

A thrill laced her treacherous spine when he pressed his cheek to hers.

'You put me under an enchantment.'

She shivered at the whispered words, although the actual words barely registered, not when his breath was hot against her ear, hot enough to seep through her skin and melt her bones.

Then, just as suddenly as he'd trapped her, he stepped away. *'Sygnomi,'* he muttered.

Legs like noodles, Tabitha kept her back propped against the wall for support and watched, dazed, as he turned his back and ran his fingers through his hair.

She had never known silence could be so charged.

He kept his back to her. 'Were you really a virgin?'

'Yes.' She'd gone to an all-girls boarding school, had looked forward to starting university and finally being able to mix with men, only to find herself homeless before she'd finished her boarding school education and having to work her fingers to the bone to make ends meet, leaving no time for *any* kind of life.

His broad shoulders rose and she heard him inhale deeply. 'And you really are pregnant?'

'Yes.'

He muttered something in his native tongue she didn't understand but which, judging by the tone, she guessed was a curse. She didn't want to know if it was aimed at herself or the situation.

Resisting the strong urge to step over and place a hand on his shoulder, she took a deep breath and tightened her ponytail with shaking hands.

The effect of his touch still blazed through her body. Her lips still tingled from the anticipated kiss that had never come. If she strained her ears she'd be able to hear the electricity still crackling through the tense silence between them.

As hard as it was, she had to ignore the tumult of feelings just sharing his air evoked in her. Tabitha might have been a virgin until their night together but she wasn't naïve. She knew sexual awareness did not automatically equate to emotional feelings. Many people were capable of having physical affairs without emotional intimacy.

She'd just never thought she would be one of them.

The times when she'd allowed herself to think of a future where she could drag herself out of the drudgery of her life and find happiness, she'd always imagined it with a faceless man and a handful of children. She'd imagined happiness. Laughter. Love.

All the things that had been denied her since

her father had died and her stepmother's true nature had come out.

All the things that had got her out of bed at the crack of dawn every day, working so hard her hands were red and sore, the tips of her fingers calloused and cracked. Dreams of a future.

Those dreams were the only thing that had stopped her spiralling into a pit of despair.

At first it had been a matter of survival but what use was surviving if there was nothing else? She'd had to believe there was something else out there for her.

And now she had to believe there was something else out there for the tiny life growing in her belly. This man with whom she shared this most inexplicable of attractions had created a life with her. He had the means and the power to give their child a life without poverty.

Giannis turned back to face her, breathing heavily.

For a long moment all they did was stare at each other.

Tabitha straightened her shoulders. 'What happens now? Do you want me to go and buy another pregnancy test? Only, I need to get back to work soon.'

His eyes narrowed dangerously and his brow furrowed.

'You can't sack me,' she said with a bluntness that belied the knots in her belly. 'I don't expect any help from you until the baby's born but I still need to support myself. I need to eat, a place to sleep… At some point I'll need to buy maternity clothes. I can't do that without an income. I have little savings. If you sack me, I'll be homeless.' She tightened her ponytail again to mask her agitation. 'All I want is for you to let me keep my job until I can legally take maternity leave. Hopefully I'll have found somewhere to live by—'

'No.' Giannis gritted his teeth and swallowed the bile rising up his throat. His guts were churning acid. All these things were happening within him but stronger than the rest was the sick compulsion to touch her, to keep touching her, to make her his again. Every part of him ached to drag her back into his arms, the few moments spent with his back to her, trying to take back control of the desire raging through him, fruitless. 'You are not returning to your duties here. You're coming to Santorini with me.'

She stared at him, the soft, full lips open but no words coming out.

'I cannot leave you here knowing you might be carrying my child.'

Could it be true? Was there a child of his loins forming within the softness of the stomach he had kissed every inch of?

'I thought you didn't believe me,' she whispered, cornflower eyes not leaving his face.

'A visit to an obstetrician will prove if you're pregnant and give a good indication of conception.'

He knew that first-hand. It was how he'd discovered it was not possible he'd fathered Anastasia's child.

But there was a big difference, he had to acknowledge. His suspicions that Tabitha had been a virgin had been confirmed. He'd read stories about women selling their virginity to the highest bidder. Was this a different version of the same thing? A woman giving her virginity to a rich man with the express desire to get pregnant?

Her virginity was the only thing he would allow himself to believe. He'd been cuckolded and humiliated once. His pride had been wounded far more than his heart and he would never put himself in that position again. It was the reason he'd decided that his next wife would be chosen using cold, hard logic.

It made his guts twist to remember how the morning after he'd thought that Tabitha might be the woman for him. She'd fitted all his requirements and the desire between them had been off the charts.

But she hadn't. She was nothing but a liar. She didn't have the independent wealth he required his next wife to have as a form of surety that she wasn't a gold-digger.

The only truth had been the desire between them and that desire had proved itself to be dangerous. It had driven him to become carried away and forget to use a condom until it had been almost too late.

Had it been too late? Tabitha was twenty-two. Helena, the second-oldest of his sisters, had fallen pregnant within a month of her marriage at the age of twenty-one. Giannis remembered his mother's delighted comment that it was because she was in the prime fertile years of her life.

He could not allow this attraction to cloud his thinking any more than it already had. He'd been led by 'feelings' before and had vowed, as he'd watched his wife and her child be lowered into the cold ground, that he would not be made a fool of again.

He looked hard at the woman who had already fooled him once with her deception. He could never trust her and he could not trust the feeling in his guts that she spoke the truth.

Giannis hadn't taken anything on trust in five years. He liked proof. Cold, hard facts.

'You will come to Santorini with me and meet with my sister's obstetrician,' he said, voicing his thoughts as he decided them.

'Aren't there obstetricians in Vienna?'

'This is one of the best obstetricians in Europe. If you are carrying my child he will be the one to monitor you throughout the pregnancy and deliver it.'

'Hold your horses.' Her hand shot out, palm up, dark, angry colour slashing her cheeks. 'Ten minutes ago you thought I was lying to you.'

'If you told me it was raining I would put my head out of the window to check. I'm still to be convinced about the pregnancy, but you would have to be the most audacious of fools to try and pretend something so easily disproved.'

'And you would have to be the most audacious of arrogant twonks to think I would let you decide anything on my behalf!'

'It's my money that will be paying for it. You, by your own admission, don't even have a home of your own to raise a child.' Ignoring her splutters of outrage, he continued, 'If things are as you say, a visit to the obstetrician will confirm it. Once it has been confirmed we can move things forward. I will put you up for the duration of the pregnancy and pay for all your expenses. If, however, the obstetrician proves that you're lying...' He smiled. 'You can find your own way home.'

The dark colour on her cheeks had drained away. She took a step back and wrapped her arms around her stomach. 'I didn't have to tell you. I could have kept the baby a secret. You could have seen me every day in this hotel and you would never have recognised me because you would never have deigned to look at a lowly worker like me. I told you because...'

'You needed my money,' he supplied sardonically.

'And because I thought you had a right to know. You might be a gazillionaire but that does not give you the right to use your money as a weapon.'

'I can use my money however I see fit. But I'm not using it as weapon, I am merely giving you my terms. If you are convinced I am the father of your child, then you can have no objection to accompanying me to Santorini. If you want the best for the child you claim is mine then I fail to see how you can object to spending the pregnancy living in luxury with the best medical attention on hand if it is needed.'

Oh, she could object, all right, Tabitha thought, panic clawing at her throat as she recognised that he was serious. He wanted to take her to Santorini. Once he had her on his home turf she would be trapped. She had enough in her bank account to fly back to Vienna but she had no doubt there would be no job to return to and that no references would be provided.

She could fly back to England but where would she go? Back to the small hotel whose owners had taken pity on her when her stepmother had first thrown her out? Back to the tiny room too small for even the least discerning guest where there was no space for a cot? And that was if that tiny room wasn't being used by someone else.

She rolled her shoulders and tried to clear the panic away to think clearly.

Giannis's offer was more generous than she could have hoped. He was giving her a way to get through the pregnancy without having to worry about finances or worry about the physical aspects of her job harming the baby the further into the pregnancy she got. What woman wouldn't want to be under the care of a top obstetrician in her first pregnancy?

So what if he didn't believe her? She couldn't expect him to take her word on trust, not after the lies by omission she'd told at the ball.

What was there to be so afraid of?

They would fly to Santorini and the obstetrician would confirm that everything she'd said was true. She had nothing to lose by going with him and everything to gain for her baby.

So why was she so afraid?

'Well?' he asked, folding his arms across his chest and staring at her with an imperious expression that made her heart ache for the generous lover who had swept her off her feet. 'What are you going to do?'

'I'm coming with you.'

He looked at his watch. 'Then I suggest you pack your belongings. We leave in two hours.'

Giannis wrapped up the meeting with his senior management team much quicker than he usually did.

He'd hardly paid attention to a word that had been exchanged.

His gut was telling him loud and clear that he was going to be a father. This was the same gut that had told him loud and clear that he was not the father of Anastasia's baby.

Striding back to his office, he went straight to his computer and clicked on the hotel's staff files. Every current member of staff was listed on it alphabetically by surname.

He didn't know Tabitha's surname.

He found her quickly, though. Tabitha Brigstock. A quick scan of the other names showed this to be the only Tabitha, which was not surprising. Tabitha was not a common name. He clicked on her name and brought up her file, which contained a copy of her résumé, a copy of her contract, copies of her appraisals and a file of all the shifts she'd undertaken over the past ninety days.

He clicked on the résumé first. His brow creased as he scanned the sparse information. It contained her full name, Tabitha Louisa Brigstock, her date of birth—her twenty-third birthday was approaching—and her employment history. There were no educational qualifications listed. She'd spent four years working as a cleaner and evening waitress at a hotel in Northamptonshire which he'd never heard of. The owner of the hotel was named as a referee. The other referee was a name he recognised—his current Head of Housekeeping, Rachel.

He brought Rachel's file up and found that she'd started working here when he'd first turned it into a hotel. Her previous employment had been at Tabitha's old hotel. Tabitha's employment in Vienna had coincided with Rachel's promotion. He deduced that Rachel had been the one to encourage Tabitha's move from England to Vienna.

He then clicked on Tabitha's contract which had been signed six months ago. She was contracted to work thirty-five hours a week as a chambermaid at a subsidised rate to account for her living in the staff quarters.

On the file listing all the shifts she'd undertaken, his eyes widened to see she worked an average of seventy-hour weeks, often covering evening housekeeping shifts and occasionally filling in at the hotel bar and restaurant. She obviously grabbed any overtime she could get.

He thought back to when he'd touched her fingers and had been surprised to find them hard and worn.

Her fingers should have been a warning sign that she wasn't who she claimed to be, he thought ruefully, smothering the ache coursing through him to imagine the long, back-breaking days Tabitha spent working herself into exhaustion. He had never encountered a woman in his social circle whose hands weren't looked after with the same zeal as her face.

On a whim, he typed her name into a search engine. No immediate matching results came up.

A knock on his office door took his attention away from any further Internet search.

He cleared his throat, his heart suddenly setting off at a canter. 'Come in.'

The door opened and, as expected, Tabitha appeared.

Her honey-blonde hair loose and impossibly long, much longer than he remembered, she'd changed out of her work uniform into a pair of slim-fitting jeans and a T-shirt that must once have been black but was so worn it had faded to a dark grey.

For some reason his heart wrenched to see it.

It was like looking at a beautiful butterfly with its old, faded cocoon still attached to it.

She carried an oversized sports bag, its strap hooked over her shoulder. Like her T-shirt, the bag was obviously well worn.

'You're still here, then,' she said lightly, pushing the door shut with her bottom. Only the tremor in her voice showed her nonchalance was nothing but a façade. 'I thought you might have run off.'

'Running off is your department.'

She winced and dropped her gaze to the floor. It was a long few moments before she lifted her head to look at him. 'I never apologised for that, did I? I'm sorry. I panicked. I was going to be late for work and I didn't know what I could say to explain myself without giving myself away.'

A boulder had lodged itself in Giannis's throat. He couldn't speak for it.

She didn't seem to expect a response, putting

her bag on the sofa on which she'd sat earlier when she'd told him she was pregnant.

She unzipped it and pulled a black item out.

He didn't notice her hands were shaking until she carried the item to him and placed it on his desk.

It was his shirt from the ball.

'I need to apologise for taking this. It was a spur-of-the-moment thing. I never meant to keep it.'

Curiosity got the better of him. 'Why did you take it?'

'It was easier to put on and escape in than my ball gown.'

'Did you escape through the bedroom window?'

She gave a sheepish nod. 'I'm sorry. And I'm sorry for not giving it back. I couldn't think how to without giving myself away.'

He leaned forward to take the shirt. Then he got to his feet and, without any ceremony, dropped it in the waste bin. 'Are you packed?'

Her eyes darted from the bin back to him. 'Yes.'

'Where's the rest of your stuff?'

She patted the bag. 'It's all in here.'

'Everything?'

She nodded. 'I've given my work uniforms back.'

A whole life enclosed in one oversized sports bag?

For some reason, his heart made that wrenching feeling again, although why that should be he didn't know, not when Tabitha didn't seem to think there was anything strange in having all her worldly possessions contained in one bag.

Not his concern, he told himself sternly. *She* was not his concern.

The only thing that should concern him was the child she purported to carry.

He would know in the morning if the child was his.

CHAPTER SIX

TABITHA LOWERED HERSELF into the biggest bath she'd ever bathed in and closed her eyes as the warmth of the foamy water enveloped her.

It was hard to believe that only eight hours ago she'd knocked on Giannis's office door, sick with apprehension.

Everything that had passed since then had gone at warp speed. Their confrontation. His ultimatum. Packing her belongings. The silent journey in the back of the chauffeured car to the airport. The flight from Vienna to Santorini in Giannis's private plane, Giannis studiously working on his laptop, Tabitha dozing but not sleeping—she'd been too overwrought to sleep. The chauffeured drive from the private airfield they'd landed in to his home... One continuous blur with no time to get her bearings and no privacy to think.

She had privacy now, though.

Giannis had left her at the entrance of his breathtakingly beautiful home saying his housekeeper, Zoe, would show her to her designated room and provide her with anything she needed. She hadn't seen or heard from him since.

She'd walked through the vast, cavernous rooms of his clifftop home with its thick, white walls feeling like she'd slipped through the looking glass.

One minute she'd been in the beautiful city of Vienna, speaking a language she'd learned at school and in which she'd become able to converse fluently, the next on what could be the most beautiful island in the whole of Europe. The sun had begun its descent when they'd arrived, the sky a glorious deep orange shining enough light to showcase the pristine white homes they'd driven past, the architecture like nowhere she'd been before.

The looking-glass feeling had continued when she'd tried to speak to Zoe, who'd taken her straight to her room. The housekeeper didn't speak a word of English. Greek was not a language on the Beddingdales curriculum so Tabitha had been stuck. Her stomach had kept rumbling but she'd been too shy and feeling too out of place to find the kitchen and communicate her hunger.

The room she'd been given was lovely, though, dual aspect windows giving her a fabulous view of the Aegean Sea now glinting under the stars of the moonless night sky. Her *en suite* bathroom had been stocked with all the toiletries a woman could need, a soft white robe hanging on its door.

She was tying the sash of the robe around her waist after she'd got out of the bath and dried herself when she heard a knock on the bedroom door.

Hurrying through the bedroom to open it, her heart leapt into her throat to find Giannis standing there.

From the dampness of his hair and the fresh, spicy scents seeping off him, he'd showered or bathed recently too. He'd also changed out of his business suit, his muscular body wrapped in a pair of casual tan chinos and a short-sleeved khaki shirt unbuttoned at the throat.

His eyes flickered over her robed form, a pulse in them that hardened to stone when he met her gaze.

'Are you going to bed?' he asked stiffly.

Suddenly feeling as naked as she was beneath the robe, she pulled the sash tighter, painfully aware of the heat engulfing her face. 'No, I've just had a bath.'

There was the slightest flare of his nostrils before his jaw tightened. 'Are you hungry?'

Her stomach rumbled loudly in answer.

It was the most mortifying sound she'd ever heard and her cheeks flamed brighter for it.

'Dinner will be brought to you in five minutes.'

'I have to eat in my room?' What was she? A prisoner?

'I've spoken to the obstetrician,' he said, ignoring her question. 'He's flying to the island first thing to meet us at his clinic here. We'll leave at eight. Do you need a wake-up call?'

'I'll set the alarm clock on my phone.'

He nodded. 'I'll see you in the morning. Goodnight.'

And as suddenly as he'd appeared, he left, heading off down the wide corridor and disappearing from sight.

Giannis got into the back of his car, his head swimming.

He could still hear the baby's fledgling heartbeat ringing in his ears.

Neither he nor Tabitha had exchanged a single

word since the obstetrician had confirmed the pregnancy. And confirmed the conception date to a narrow period which coincided exactly with the date of the ball.

As much as he would like to think Tabitha was the sort of woman who could lose her virginity to a man one day and sleep with another the next, he just could not see it.

His gut had been right. He was going to be a father.

Resting his head back against the soft leather upholstery, he closed his eyes.

'Are you okay?'

Tabitha's softly spoken words soaked through him.

He jerked a nod.

He'd hoped for a different outcome. He'd hoped the visit would result in him driving Tabitha back to the airport and never having to see her again.

But he could not deny that the confirmation had delivered a bolt of pure joy inside him. There had been a moment when he'd had to fist his hands to stop himself from leaning over to kiss her.

Every moment with her was a fight against himself not to touch her.

The spell she'd woven over him a month ago still lived in his blood. He'd felt it on the flight from Vienna when he'd worked diligently on his laptop but found his attention wrapped solely in the woman reclining on the seat opposite him, sleeping. He'd felt it on the drive to his home, felt it sharpen at the shine in her eyes when she'd seen his home, then felt it burst through his veins when she'd opened her bedroom door, wearing nothing but a robe and a cloud of her divine scent.

The evening meal he'd planned to share with her...

A snap judgement had decided for him that it would be better if she ate alone.

Merely sharing the same air as her did things to him that could not be explained by any degree of logic.

His desire for Tabitha was like a sickness and he had to treat it as such. To touch her and make love to her again would only drag him further into her duplicitous web.

And now that delectable temptation would be under his nose for the next eight months. If he didn't take drastic action she would be a permanent part of his life, this woman in whose web he'd foolishly allowed himself to be caught.

'Name your price,' he said heavily.

'My price for what?'

'For me to have sole custody of our child. Name it. Cash. Property. Whatever you want.'

She was silent for the longest time.

His heart thudded as he awaited her response.

When she finally answered there was an iciness to her tone he had never heard from her before. 'That is the most offensive thing I have ever heard.'

'Why? You are not in a position to raise a child. You have nothing. I can give our child everything it desires and the best education money can buy.'

'Are you saying that being poor disqualifies me from being a good parent?'

'You cannot tell me that you want a child,' he said roughly, ignoring her question. Of course he didn't believe that. He remembered the old Basinas family gardener who'd had three children he'd doted on. They'd lived hand to mouth in a tiny home but they'd been the happiest kids he'd known, secure and loved. He'd loved playing with them when he'd been a child and still kept in touch with them as an adult.

He also knew plenty of rich people who were lousy parents and whose children were spoilt brats.

None of this was the issue. The issue was Tabitha, this duplicitous temptress, who even now had every cell in his body singing for her. 'You're young, single, you have no home, no money...'

'That last issue can easily be resolved by child support from you, which I will be legally entitled to. I'm young but I'm not a child—'

'What can you inspire a child to be?' he interrupted, knowing even as the words came out that they were cruel, but unable to stop them, the determination to talk Tabitha out of his life far stronger than decency and compassion. 'I've seen your résumé—what qualifications do you have? I assume you have none, seeing as you did not list them. Or do I have that wrong?'

'What do qualifications have to do with raising a child?' she hissed indignantly. 'Children need one thing only—love. To say only the best educated and those with a disposable income are the only people capable of raising a child well is unspeakably snobbish and cruel.'

'Anyone can love a child,' he conceded. 'But, if it came to a choice between love and a roof over their head, every child would choose the roof.'

'Twaddle. I lost my mum when I was a little girl. If you'd asked me then if I would prefer to live in a big, swanky house or have my mother I would have chosen my mother every time. I would have happily lived in a cardboard box if it had meant having her with me.

'And,' she continued before her words about her mother could really penetrate and before he could get a word in, 'I take umbrage with your assertion that anyone can love a child. There are people on this earth—rich people, poor people—who shouldn't be allowed within a thousand miles of one. I will not give you custody of our child, not now or ever, and if you ever make such a suggestion again you will never see me or our child again.'

If they hadn't been in the back of a moving car, Tabitha would have stormed off.

She resisted the urge to kick the seat opposite her and resisted the even stronger temptation to kick Giannis.

Instead, she twisted so her back was to him and looked out of the window at the passing scenery, breathing hard to regulate the tumultuous emotions rippling through her.

Her heart ached to think of the generous lover under whose spell she had fallen for one magical night. He had been warm.

This man was cold.

This man hated her.

He hated her so much that he'd made her dine in her room alone rather than share his evening dinner or breakfast with her. He hated her so much that rather than allow the sound of their baby's heartbeat to bond them together as parents, if not allies, he had stabbed her heart with his cruel offer to pay for her to abandon the life growing inside her.

What would he have done if she'd said yes—locked her away while the baby incubated inside her as if she were livestock?

Nausea cramped in her stomach and she put a protective hand to it.

Give up her child? She would rather die.

They had made this life together but the truth was Giannis didn't think she was good enough to be a mother to his child. She'd been good enough to sleep with when he'd assumed she was wealthy but now he knew the truth of her circumstances he wanted nothing to do with her. He didn't want to touch her, didn't want to look at her.

She didn't want him to touch her, she told herself defiantly. If he was so shallow that he judged a person's worth on their income and job title then he could go stick his head up his backside.

She heard him shift in his seat and caught a whiff of his cologne.

Her heart ballooned as fresh awareness raced through her, moving too fast for her to take any kind of control over it and squash it back in a box where it belonged.

Pressing her forehead to the window, she stared miserably at the pristine white homes they were driving past.

She didn't want his touch. She didn't.

This sick awareness of him was not her choice and how she could still feel it was beyond reason. Even now, sitting here, despising him and despising his cold cruelty, her senses were alert to his closeness. She'd lain on the obstetrician's medical bed and rolled her T-shirt up over her belly, had the sonographer place the cold gel onto her skin and, until the moment the tiny blob that was her growing child had appeared on the screen, had been consumed with Giannis's presence. When the first sound of a heartbeat had rung out in the small consulting room, their eyes had met for the only time since leaving his home that morning, and for one beautiful moment she'd experienced a connection with him that had filled her with so many emotions she'd wanted to throw her arms around him, press her head to his chest and hear his heartbeat too.

All her hopes that they could find an agreement to be amicable co-parents had evaporated.

A prickle on the back of her neck told her Giannis was looking at her.

A moment later his deep voice cut through the silence. 'If you ever threaten to take my child away from me again, I will sue you for full custody. And I will win.'

His cold words almost knocked the air from her lungs.

Inhaling deeply, she clenched her hands into fists. 'Don't treat me and my child like a commodity and I won't have to make that threat. Oh, and I wasn't threatening you—I was promising.

Take me to court. See how a judge reacts to you throwing your money around to buy a baby.'

She heard his own sharp intake of breath.

When he next spoke, it sounded as if it were coming from between tightly gritted teeth. 'I was merely trying to think of the best way to proceed—the best way for all our interests.'

'All *your* interests, you mean. If I was as shallow and money-grabbing as you keep implying, I would have accepted your offer and you wouldn't have to face a future explaining to all and sundry that the mother of your child is a chambermaid. You could say the child was conceived by a surrogate.'

His phone suddenly vibrated in his pocket. He pulled it out and saw it was Niki.

He sighed and switched it off without answering. His youngest sister was furious with him for abandoning her in Vienna, although there was some debate as to whether 'abandoning' was the correct term, considering he'd put her in the best suite of the hotel and sent his plane back to collect her that morning. He was not ready to tell her or any of his family about Tabitha. Not when he was still trying to get to grips with the situation.

It was a situation he knew his family would be delighted about. He also knew what they would expect him to do about it. They would expect him to marry her.

His driver turned onto the long driveway that took them to Giannis's home. Staring out of the window at the home he loved and had expected to be filled with children long before now, an overwhelming weariness flooded through him, and he bowed his head and rubbed the back of his neck.

'I've appointments in Athens to get to. I'll be back later this evening. We can discuss the situation more then.'

He reached out to touch the honey-blonde hair splaying down her back and over her seat and pulled his hand back with only inches to spare.

He needed some legal advice because the only future he could see now involved marrying this woman who evoked the stickiest desire he'd ever known and a maelstrom of emotions in him. If marriage was the route they needed to take then he needed to get a grip on it all. And fast.

With the sun already blazing high in the azure sky, Tabitha rolled her jeans up her calves as far she could and put a black vest on. It was the closest thing to beach wear she could create from her limited wardrobe.

Then she walked down the long pebbled steps that led from Giannis's clifftop house to his private beach. She'd just reached the bottom of them when Giannis's housekeeper came tearing after her with a bottle of sunscreen and a large bottle of water.

Touched at the thoughtful gesture, and wishing she could thank the kind woman in her language, she kissed her cheek as a means of conveying her gratitude.

Alone with nothing but the clear Aegean Sea, she sank onto the dark volcanic sand and, for the first time in over four years, spent a day doing nothing. No cleaning. No washing. No scrubbing. No ironing. She just sat on the beach with the sun toasting her skin and got lost in her thoughts.

Slowly her fury at Giannis's offer to effectively buy their baby from her lessened but threads of agitation grew in its place. He wanted to talk more about the 'situation' later.

What would happen to her now? What would happen to her baby? She wished desperately that her father were still alive. Just a warm embrace from him would be enough. He'd been such a good man, always wanting the best for his only child. It would have devastated him to see what had become of her. It would have devastated him to learn the wife he'd chosen with such care for his daughter's sake had been a wolf in sheep's clothing. He'd known Tabitha's relationship with her stepsisters hadn't been the loving one he'd envisaged but he'd never dreamed the rot went all the way to the top. If he had, he would never have put his second wife down as a trustee to his estate. He would have better protected Tabitha.

Would Giannis only want the best for their child? He'd implied as much but what did his interpretation of 'best' even mean? Did it only mean material things? Or did it include love and affection?

His assertion that she had nothing to offer a child had stung but not as much as his cruel question as to how she could inspire their child.

Giannis looked at her and saw an insignificant nobody.

She wished it didn't make her heart ache so much to know that that was who she'd become.

But now she needed to become someone. She needed to be the mother her child deserved.

Giannis took a deep breath before knocking on Tabitha's door.

A long day had been broken up with a quick chat with his lawyer, who'd confirmed marriage was the most sensible route to take if he wanted any rights over his child. The law in Greece gave unmarried mothers sole custody. He would only have rights to his child if Tabitha consented. He could take her to court. With the legal minds he would employ, he could be reasonably certain of winning, but there were no guarantees in life. Marriage cut out any risks. He would be his child's legal parent in the eyes of the law and seamlessly solve any future problem regarding custody and maintenance.

Marriage protected him. The sooner he tied Tabitha down the better, before she learned for herself that she held three out of the four aces in the pack. Which meant he needed to go on a charm offensive.

The door opened slowly.

When their eyes met he had a moment where all thoughts flew from his brain.

She looked dishevelled in rolled-up jeans and a black vest top, her pretty feet bare, long honey-blonde hair tumbling messily over her shoulders.

She tucked a lock of it behind her ear, colour rising on her rounded cheekbones.

Damn it, even resembling a grubby urchin she was beautiful.

There was a smudge on her left cheek. He rammed his hand into his pocket to stop himself from reaching out to wipe it clean.

His beautiful liar was the greatest temptation he had ever known. That made her more dangerous than she could understand.

But she was here, in his home, under his roof. If he wanted his rights to the child growing beneath the stomach that looked only a little rounder since their night together to be guaranteed, he needed to marry her. To marry her, he needed her consent.

He cleared his throat. 'Dinner will be served for us on the terrace in twenty minutes.'

There was not the slightest softening on the beautiful stony face before him. 'You want to eat with me?'

No. He never wanted to be near her again, never have that astounding beauty in his sight, never have her scent dive into his senses, never hear that fake cut-glass but utterly melodious, husky voice, never have his own fingers itch to reach out and touch the soft skin he so vividly remembered the texture and taste of…

Loins thickening uncomfortably, he gave a sharp nod and stepped back. 'I'll meet you out there.'

Then he turned and headed straight to his own room at the other end of his home to the room he'd put her in, far out of the reach of temptation.

Standing under the shower, he knew he had to get a grip. If she did consent to marry him then the temptation that was Tabitha would no longer be a temptation. She would be his wife. She would share his bed. Share his life.

Frustrated and furious with himself for his weakness around her, he punched the wall.

Damn it to hell, how had he got so carried away that he'd failed to put the condom on before thrusting inside her?

But that was the wrong question to ask because all it did was make his already aching loins remember the exquisite pleasure of being bare inside her.

CHAPTER SEVEN

WHEN GIANNIS ARRIVED at the terrace he found the table set as he'd instructed but no Tabitha.

Pouring himself a large glass of white wine, he took a seat and waited.

She appeared ten minutes later in the same rolled-up jeans and black vest she'd answered her bedroom door in, her hair brushed, her face clean but her cheeks flushed. 'Sorry. I got lost.'

Awareness stabbed through him so hard that all he could do was raise a brow.

Her nerves came out in her voice. 'I thought you meant the terrace at the back with the swimming pool. I didn't know there was one overlooking the beach too. It's very well hidden.'

'It's secluded,' he agreed. 'Please, sit. Would you like a drink?'

'Just water, please.' Tabitha took the seat she assumed had been set for her—judging by the cutlery setting, they were having a three-course meal—and looked out at the magnificent view so as to avoid meeting his eye again until her heart had slowed to a more manageable beat.

Trying desperately to distract herself, she inhaled the fragrant floral air mingled with the scent of the sea that glimmered before her. This terrace had to be right below her bedroom.

The more she explored Giannis's home, the more there was to discover, including that the vast majority of it was carved into the cliff itself.

He poured water for her from a jug and indicated the pitta bread and dips already laid on the table.

Being alone with him had killed her appetite quicker than the gory pictures her stepsisters had liked to show her to scare her when she was a child but this was a much different appetite suppressant. This suppressant was because large butterflies had suddenly formed in her stomach, their wings fluttering hard all the way up to her throat.

Although she knew she wouldn't be able to manage more than a small amount, Tabitha dipped some of the bread into the pink *taramasalata* and took a tiny bite.

Giannis was the one to break the silence. 'Forgive me for not asking this sooner, but how are you finding the pregnancy?'

She swallowed her bite-sized morsel and forced herself to look at him. 'Exciting and frightening.'

'That is understandable. What about physically? Have you noticed any changes?'

'I suffer with afternoon morning sickness.' She managed a small smile to see the furrow in his brow. 'Every afternoon, without fail, I get nauseous. I've learned to only eat plain food for lunch then it's less severe but, either way, it doesn't last long—an hour or so. I also get tired easily but that's it. So far, so good.'

She crossed her legs to stop the jitters.

Why were they pretending? Why was *she* pretending? Pretending that sharing a meal with Giannis was normal, that she wasn't suspicious at this change in attitude towards her? She wanted to be thankful for it but she couldn't. When he'd dropped her back at his home earlier he'd hardly been able to look her in the eye. Now he was pouring her drinks on the terrace of his home, sharing a meal in a setting that could only be considered as romantic.

'Maybe the sea air here will help with the sickness,' he observed.

'Maybe. I was nauseous earlier but I wasn't sick.'

'That's encouraging.' He dipped a large chunk of pitta into the humus and popped it whole into his mouth.

Unable to take this stilted, fake politeness a moment longer, she wiped her fingers on the cotton napkin and raised her chin. 'Why are you being nice to me?'

He didn't pretend not to know what she was talking about. He took hold of his glass but, instead of drinking from it, he swirled the wine within it. 'I have been harsh with you. For that I apologise. The news about your pregnancy came as a shock but now we have to move forward...'

Before Giannis could finish and tell her he thought they should marry, there came the sound of clacking footsteps followed by his sister Niki bursting through the French doors.

'What are you doing here?' he asked in Greek, rising from his chair.

'To tell you off. You left me in Vienna without a word of explanation and have been avoiding all my calls since.' She cast a beady stare at Tabitha. 'Is *she* the reason for...?'

But then Niki cut herself off and stared even harder at her with widening eyes. 'Tabitha?'

Giannis watched as recognition flickered in the cornflower eyes. 'Niki?'

'You two know each other?' His mind raced. His sister had not spent a great deal of time at his palace hotel but she was a gregarious soul who made friends easily. It would be just like her to befriend a chambermaid.

An enormous smile spread over Niki's face and, in English, she said, 'It *is* you! What are you doing here? How do you know my brother?'

The shock on Tabitha's face told its own story. 'Giannis is your *brother*?'

Niki beamed and nodded, then pulled out a chair to sit, uninvited.

'How do you two know each other?' Giannis asked again, his curiosity outweighing his frustration at this rude interruption.

Grabbing Tabitha's unused wine glass, Niki poured herself a glass. 'Tabitha was at Beddingdales with Simone, Melina's cousin. We used to meet up at weekends if we had the same leave.'

Melina was Niki's best friend. Melina had been the reason Niki had refused to go to Beddingdales herself, begging their parents to send her to the same English boarding school that Melina was being sent to. As Niki could wrap her parents around her little finger, they'd agreed.

But none of this was what Giannis was thinking of.

He stared at Tabitha, met her expressionless gaze and felt the ground shift beneath him.

Then Niki burst into a peel of laughter. 'I've just realised—you're the woman who took Giannis's attention for the whole of the masquerade ball! I was sure you were familiar but with your mask on I couldn't place where I knew you from!'

He whipped his head round to look at his sister.

She'd mentioned his 'mystery woman' a couple of times in the days after the ball but not once had she said the woman in question was familiar to her. After he had shut her up about the subject, she had stopped mentioning it.

If he had known Tabitha had rung a bell with Niki he would have made her think hard about who she could be.

He looked again at the woman carrying his child.

How the hell did a girl from one of the world's most exclusive and expensive all-girls boarding schools grow into a woman so impoverished she'd become a live-in chambermaid?

The next hour passed with Tabitha in a daze.

Niki was Giannis's sister? She'd never known her well but had always remembered her, mostly because she was one of the most fun people she'd ever met. A few years older than Tabitha, she'd exuded a glamour Tabitha would have killed to achieve for herself. Whenever she'd come with Melina to visit Simone in the town near their school, Tabitha had been thrilled to be included in the group.

Whether she was oblivious to the tension in the air or whether she just chose to ignore it, only Niki knew, but she stayed, happily helping herself to Tabitha's leftovers, of which there were many, from all the delicious courses they were served. There were many instances of, 'Do you remember?' to which Tabitha would nod and smile but chatterbox Niki didn't require input from either of them. From the way her merry eyes darted between them, she obviously thought they'd got together at the ball and had been seeing each other in secret since.

When she finally took one of the enormous

hints Giannis kept dropping and said her good-byes—and Giannis insisted on seeing her out, most likely to ensure she actually left—Tabitha got to her feet and stood at the thick white wall that acted as a barrier between the terrace and sheer drop beneath them.

She breathed in deeply, inhaling the wonderful night scents, trying hard to compose herself.

Something was about to happen. She could feel it in her bones: an anticipation.

But whether it was an anticipation of dread she couldn't tell. Whatever it was, she needed to keep herself together. She needed to be strong.

His footsteps were heavy when he joined her back on the terrace.

He poured himself another glass of wine from the second bottle to be opened after Niki had demolished most of the first one and drank half of it before putting the glass on the table and coming over to stand beside her.

The night sky and the romantic lights illuminating the terrace cast his handsome face in shadows that gave him a gothic, piratical look. It made her heart ache, reminding her strongly of how he had looked the night of the ball when she had fallen under his spell.

The heady awareness that lived in her blood for him flickered to life with all the ease of a switch. Without the barrier of the table between them he was close enough to touch.

For a long time he stared at her with a hard curiosity. 'Who are you?'

She forced herself to maintain eye contact. 'Are you asking because you saw me as a dirt-poor chambermaid and assumed that's all I ever was?'

His eyes narrowed. 'I never thought that.'

'Didn't you?' she challenged. 'I saw the shock in your eyes when Niki said how she knew me. You assumed I lied about Beddingdales, didn't you? You were so confident it was a lie, you never bothered to ask. You didn't think a privately educated woman could possibly get her hands dirty working in domestic service. It was easier to assume I was a liar than give me the benefit of the doubt.'

'If I thought you a liar, it's because you lied about your identity to get into the ball. You lied about who you were,' he ground out.

'The only lie was the name on the invitation I entered the ball with. I told you my real name. I told you I worked in hospitality, which was stretching the truth, I admit, but it was the closest I could get without telling a lie. Everything else was the truth. I was an imposter that night but I'm not a liar, Giannis, whatever you may think of me.'

His lips thinned, a pulse throbbing on his jawline. 'You made assumptions too. You ran out on me without giving me a chance. You didn't even attempt to tell me the truth. You assumed that I would be furious that you worked for me and sack you.'

'With good reason.' Tabitha held her ground and tried to hold on to her train of thought which was threatening to slip away. His spicy scent had slowly mingled with the fragrant bougainvillea and was seeping through her airwaves with every inhalation. If she stretched out her hand, she would reach his chest. Her hand was begging her to do just that. 'And you proved it when you tried to sack me the moment you realised I worked for you.'

'I'd spent…' He cut himself off and ran his fingers roughly through his hair. 'I was angry. You say you didn't tell me one lie, but you let me believe you were someone you were not. Or *are* you the person you pretended to be?'

'I was that person once, but that was a long time ago, and I would say you were more than angry when I came to you and you realised I was nothing but a chambermaid. You were disgusted and don't you dare deny it—it was written all over your face.'

'I was disgusted with myself for falling for a woman who wasn't who she claimed to be. I've been there before. My wife... You know I was married?' It was a question framed as a statement.

The picture she'd seen of Giannis and his stunning wife on their wedding day flashed immediately into her mind, the way they had stared into each other's eyes... It felt like a hand had grabbed hold of her heart and twisted it.

Since she'd arrived in Santorini, Tabitha had tried hard not to think of the woman who had shared his life here before tragedy had struck, because every time she did she had the sick feeling of stepping on another woman's toes and something else, something much deeper and stomach-twisting, which she dared not think about in any depth.

But hearing him acknowledge his wife for the first time...

'Yes.' The clenching in her heart softened to imagine the hell he must have gone through losing the love of his life as he'd done. 'I'm sorry for what happened to her.'

Giannis shrugged and raised his chin.

By the time of Anastasia's death he'd grown to hate her but not as much as he'd despised himself for believing her lies.

That he felt guilt and a responsibility for her death were things he could not fathom. He hadn't been driving that car. She had.

She'd been driving it to her lover.

'I'd learned she was a gold-digger who was cheating on me.'

He watched Tabitha stiffen before he cast his eyes away from her to the dark sea before them.

Too many emotions curled through him when he looked at her. The spell she'd bewitched him with the night they'd conceived their child breathed powerfully in his blood stream, his desire for her threatening again to cloud his thoughts. How easy it would be to cup her beautiful face in his hands, plunder that enticing mouth and lose himself in the pleasure they had created together all over again.

Always he'd been the master of his desire, even during his short, ill-fated marriage.

With Tabitha he felt a breath away from losing control without even touching her.

A yacht sailed past them in the distance. He focused his attention on it, using it much like the anchor the yacht would use when it reached harbour, wherever that would be.

'Anastasia tried to pass her lover's child off as mine,' he said in as emotionless a tone as he could manage. He heard a sharp intake of breath but ignored it. 'She fell pregnant three months after we married. I should have been delighted but my gut told me something did not feel right. She had the scan done without me, only telling me about it after the fact, so I visited the obstetrician privately. I asked if the date of conception could be determined from the scan and learned that it could to a good degree of accuracy.

'The child Anastasia claimed was mine had been conceived during the ten days I was in Brazil. It was not possible I was the father. I set a private investigative team onto her and learned our entire marriage was a sham. All she wanted was my money and the lifestyle. She never wanted me.'

He could not bring himself to tell Tabitha about his confrontation with Anastasia's lover and his admission that she'd planned to leave him after the birth. Giannis would have been the legal father and liable to pay maintenance. Anastasia would also have been entitled to a good chunk of his money in her own right.

He'd just shared more with Tabitha than he had with anyone else. Not even his family knew Anastasia's child had not been his. A man had his pride.

Anastasia's actions had humiliated him. The bruises to his pride still lived in him.

But Tabitha's child was his and, whatever virulent, dangerous emotions his child's mother evoked in him, all that mattered was securing his child to his side.

'It's no secret that one of the reasons for me hosting the masquerade ball was to find a new wife,' he said into the stunned silence. 'The time was right. I'm thirty-five and I want to be a father before I'm too old to play football with my children. I wanted my next wife to be a woman who was independently wealthy. I do not want love in my next marriage—I've done love and it tastes bitter—but I wanted security in my wife's

MICHELLE SMART

motives for marrying me. You are carrying my child. It would be wrong of me not to give our child the same opportunities it would have had with the mother of my choice. As you won't countenance me having custody of our child, the next best thing is for us to marry.'

'I beg your pardon?' Tabitha must have misheard him, too dazed at his unexpected revelation about his marriage to have been listening properly.

She didn't want to feel sorry for him but she did. What a blow it must have been to a man as proud as Giannis to learn he'd been cuckolded, and what a blow to his heart too. He must have been devastated.

No wonder he'd doubted Tabitha about the pregnancy. If she'd been in his shoes she might have demanded proof too.

'I want us to marry,' he repeated.

She twisted her face to look at him but all she found was his profile gazing into the distance, his jaw clenched, hands gripping the wall tightly.

Marriage?

That feeling of having slipped through the looking glass hit her strongly again, the pebbled ground beneath her feet starting to spin. 'Marriage? You and me?'

'If you marry me, our baby will not want for anything.'

'That applies even if we don't marry,' she managed to croak. 'You would still have to pay child support.'

Of all the things she had expected him to suggest about a way forward for them as parents, not once had it crossed her mind he would suggest this.

'It is better for a child to have two parents together.' Suddenly he turned his face to her. His eyes bored into hers with an intensity she could feel right in her core. 'Marry me and our child will have a mother and father living under the same roof. Two parents available at all times. No being shunted from one home to another. No insecurities about which home is their home, no wondering which parent they are spending the weekend or school holidays with. And you would have greater security too—the law would give you that.'

'Why offer this now? Only this morning you wanted to buy our child from me and cut me from its life.' But, before he could respond, the answer came to her and all the sympathy she'd felt for him vanished. 'Coincidence, is it, that you suggest marriage within hours of learning I was privately educated? Does it make me more acceptable to your standing in your world?'

His features darkened, becoming taut. 'You insult me.'

'You insult *me*.' All the emotions she'd been trying to supress for so long, all her fears and insecurities, merged with the anger she hadn't felt creeping up on her at his cruel words, colliding to crash through her in a wave. 'You tell me you want us to marry in the same breath as telling me I'm not the woman of choice to be mother of your child. You say I don't disgust you, that my job isn't an issue…'

'It has *never* been an issue.'

'But half the time you won't even look at me!'

She'd hardly finished uttering the last word when two huge hands lunged at her and gripped her shoulders, pulling her to him. His piratical features only inches from hers, he snarled, 'Look at you? You have turned my world on its head! I am trying to navigate my way through everything, trying to do what's right and best for my child, but just sharing the same air as you distracts my thoughts. Yes, *matia mou*, I have an issue with looking at you but it's not because I'm the snob you think I am. I look at you and all I want is to throw you over my shoulder, carry you to the nearest bed and rip the clothes from your body with my teeth.'

Heart thumping, Tabitha stared into the clear blue eyes that were filled with the same anger and desire that coiled in her and felt something low inside her melt.

And then Giannis's mouth caught hers with a savage possessiveness that sent everything else inside her melting too.

Sticky warmth flooded her. The ache she'd carried inside her since the night they'd conceived their child bloomed as her senses filled with his spicy scent and dark, wine-laced taste. Wrapping her arms around him, she sank into the hungry urgency of his mouth.

One touch from Giannis was like the spark of a match on kindling: immediate and utterly combustible. And yet there was so much more than the flames licking her skin. There was a sense of rightness. Where she turned his world upside down, he righted hers. Being held in his arms… it felt as if this was where she was meant to be.

Their tongues wound together in a heady, sensuous exploration while his fingers threaded down through her long hair until he reached the base of her spine, evoking sensation that made her stomach contract and blood move relentlessly through her veins. Splaying his hand, he moulded her closer to him so the hard contours of his body were flush against hers.

She hardly noticed when his hands gripped her waist and lifted her from the ground to carry her effortlessly to the far wall covered in a tumbling display of flowers, not until her feet were placed back on the ground and she had to tighten her hold around him to stop her watery legs giving way beneath her.

His hard mouth wrenched from her lips to graze over her cheek and burrow into her neck, his hands pushing up her vest and bra, fingers brushing over her ribcage to her breasts to capture and knead the tender tips before capturing her breasts whole. A rich wave of sensation darted heavily through her sensitive flesh.

Capable fingers dragged down her belly to the button of her jeans and wrenched them open. His mouth crashed back onto hers at the same moment his fingers dipped beneath the band of her knickers and her gasp was smothered by the weight of his heady kisses.

Her body had become a playground of tingling nerves and her hips arched towards him of their own volition. When his fingers edged down through the soft curls of her pubis to the slick heat at the core of her womanhood, she writhed, helpless against the exquisite pleasure engulfing her.

The pleasure grew in intensity, a yearning growing with it, stronger, needier, reaching, searching, all of it centred on Giannis and his magical manipulations, until she reached the tipping point and she pressed her cheek to his throat and held him tightly as an explosion of rippling pleasure roared through her.

She was still awash with the waves of bliss flooding through her loins when he disentangled himself and stepped back, visibly fighting for air.

Pressing herself against the cold wall for support, she stared at him, dazed, fighting for her own breath.

His throat moved then he rubbed his head angrily.

'You see what you do to me?' he said roughly.

'How can I hate you when you make me feel like this? What you do to me...'

What she did to *him*?

Had he not just seen—*felt*—what he'd done to her?

Hands shaking, she straightened her clothes and fumbled the buttons of her jeans back up.

She couldn't speak, could only watch mutely as he strode heavily to the table and downed what was left of his wine.

He rolled his shoulders and breathed deeply before looking back at her. 'I am serious about us marrying, *matia mou*, and I want you to think seriously about it too. Sleep on it. I don't wish to fight you but be under no illusions—I will not accept anything less than being a permanent part of my child's life. All a custody battle will do is give the press a meal to feed on and line our lawyers' pockets.'

And then he left the terrace without looking back.

CHAPTER EIGHT

BY THE TIME Tabitha woke the next morning after a tumultuous night of very little sleep, she found Giannis had gone. Zoe, the housekeeper, handed her a note from him with a smile. All the note said was he had gone to work and would see her at dinner.

His absence was an unexpected mercy.

She wasn't ready to face him. Not after what had happened on his terrace.

But she couldn't deny that the sinking of her stomach at his absence felt very much like disappointment.

Back in her bedroom, she rooted through her limited wardrobe for something clean to wear that she wouldn't swelter in. In Vienna she rarely left the hotel, and normally just stuck to wearing her work uniform, so had had little need for a summer wardrobe. Or a winter wardrobe. Without that uniform, she was stuck, especially in the Santorini summer heat.

She kneaded her forehead, nauseous that she needed to spend some of her savings on something as frivolous as clothes. She had few savings as it was. If things got ugly with Giannis she would need every cent she had...

Who was she trying to kid? If things got ugly with Giannis she had no hope of fighting him. Compared to those of a normal person her savings were pitiful. Compared to a billionaire's they were laughable. He probably carried more in spare change than she had in her bank account.

After dressing in another pair of rolled-up jeans and the thinnest top she had, she left Giannis's house and headed off in the direction she remembered driving through, which led to busy streets. Unfortunately she underestimated the distance and it was a good hour before she found civilisation. By then perspiration soaked her skin and clothes and she'd drunk all the water from the bottle she'd taken.

Thirsty, she stopped at a small café packed with holiday makers—at least she'd found a tourist hotspot, and if there were holiday makers that meant shops—and ordered a large glass of lemonade and a slice of pizza.

Finding a table tucked away in the corner, she waited for her order and sank back into her thoughts.

That was all she'd done since she'd left Giannis's home. Walked and thought. Walked and thought.

Those thoughts continued to consume her as she ate her small lunch and then hunted for the shops selling cheap clothes, continued as she rifled through rows of generic beach dresses and as she tried on dress after dress, eventually settling on the cheapest two she liked the most and which might survive more than a couple of washes.

Her thoughts continued when she eventually, reluctantly, began the walk back to Giannis's home.

To raise her child in that magnificent home on this beautiful island was the stuff of dreams. Fantasies. Her child would want for nothing.

But her child would want for nothing even if she refused. Legally, Giannis would have to pay child support.

If she married him, her child would have two parents under the same roof. That was the best way to raise a child. Everyone said so.

Except Tabitha's happiest childhood memories were of when it had been just her and her father. She had only vague memories of her mother. She remembered the feeling of love and security she'd had with her and she'd always missed her, always felt a part of herself was missing, but she'd died before solid memories could form.

Her father had remarried when Tabitha had been ten. He'd introduced Emmaline as her new mother. He'd married her because he'd been lonely and because he'd believed, his own mother having since died, that his pre-pubescent daughter needed a mother. The two older stepsisters his marriage had given Tabitha were supposed to have been an additional bonus for a lonely child.

If Tabitha didn't marry Giannis that would leave him free to marry someone else who would become stepmother to her child.

A pain shot through her heart every time this particular thought entered her head and it was a pain that terrified her.

Because it wasn't just the fear of a stepmother resenting her child, as Emmaline had resented her, or fear that that resentment could become as poisonous as Emmaline's had become towards Tabitha. It wasn't the thought of Giannis with another woman that hurt. It was the thought of Giannis gazing at another woman with the same intense devotion with which he had gazed at Anastasia.

Her thoughts darkened with each step, and her legs were aching as she ascended a particularly steep narrow road. A car appeared at the crest of the hill she was walking up and her heart began to thump before her brain had even fully registered it.

It was the sports car she'd seen parked at the back of Giannis's house.

Pressing her hand to her chest, she tried to breathe through a throat that had closed.

This was the real reason she found herself shying away from doing the right thing by her child. Her attraction to its father was too strong, too overwhelming and more rooted than all the other emotions she felt towards him. She was the kindling to his flame. She had debased herself on his terrace, coming undone in his arms like a wildling, and for all his accusations about her doing things to him he hadn't been the one to lose control. She had.

She thought of the night when they had conceived their child as a magical dream. There had been a connection between them she could never explain in words but she had felt it so acutely. It had breathed through every part of her. Falling into his bed had felt like the most natural thing in the world and she had closed her ears to all the dangers because she had been caught in a spell so wonderful she hadn't wanted it to end.

That inexplicable connection was still there but it had transformed into something darker, their fledgling relationship containing something explosive and elemental that she was too inexperienced to understand.

She wished desperately that she had told him the truth instead of running out on him. He was right that she'd never given him a chance. She had made assumptions.

But if she had stayed and taken her chances with the truth then she strongly suspected the outcome would have been everything that had stopped her revealing it. He would have felt duped whether she had told him then or not.

They would never have had a chance.

The car stopped beside her. The driver's window slid down with a soft burr.

Their eyes met.

Her heart bloomed.

'Get in.'

'Sorry?'

'It's not safe for me to park here.'

Blinking furiously, she hurried round to the passenger side and climbed in. The interior smelled of leather and Giannis's spicy cologne.

He put the car in gear and they roared off.

'Where have you been?' Giannis asked tightly. The fresh air pouring in from the open window pushed away the faint trace of Tabitha's scent his greedy nostrils had detected when she'd sat beside him but that did nothing to stop his pulses reacting to her close proximity.

To distract himself some more, he pressed the button that opened the roof.

He'd called home after his second meeting to be told by his housekeeper that Tabitha had been gone for four hours. An hour later she still hadn't returned and, unable to shake the angst that gnawed away inside him, he'd cut his day short and taken the small plane he used to commute between Santorini and Athens back home. Finding that she still hadn't returned, he'd jumped in the car and set about finding her, cursing himself for not taking her phone number.

'Shopping,' she answered.

He glanced at the thin plastic bag she clutched on her lap and loosened his clenched jaw. 'You didn't tell Zoe where you were going. She was worried about you.'

'I couldn't. She doesn't speak English and I don't speak Greek.'

He looked again at the bag on her lap and swallowed back his rising temper. 'You've been gone for seven hours.'

'Am I on a curfew?'

The roof now fully open, her long hair caught in the breeze. Although he knew intellectually that he couldn't smell its fragrance, his senses reacted as if they did and he tightened his grip on the steering wheel. 'You should have told someone.'

'Told who? *None* of your staff speak English and, in any case, since when do I need to account for my movements?'

'Next time, leave a note.' He couldn't stop himself from adding, 'You haven't got much to show for seven hours' worth of shopping.'

And that cheap, thin plastic bag should not make his heart ache. All the women in his family went shopping and returned with their goods packed in pretty boxes and carried in smart designer bags.

'That's because I haven't got much money,' she retorted icily. 'Would you like a blow-by-blow account of my movements?'

'You are carrying my child.'

'And? Do you think it gives you autonomy over me?'

He sighed as he slowed for a bend and changed to a lower gear. 'I listen to you speak and I wonder how I thought you uneducated. You're quick. Literate–'

'And you're changing the subject.'

'I don't want another argument.'

His home gleamed bright on the clifftop in the near distance but, instead of taking the right turn that would have led to his driveway, he continued on the road they were already on.

Having to concentrate on the road before him meant they could talk without his thoughts being entirely consumed by ripping her clothes off.

Theos, he still couldn't get what had happened on the terrace last night from his mind. He'd had no fulfilment for himself but it hadn't mattered. Tabitha's uninhibited, wanton responses to his touch had been as heady and fulfilling as anything he had ever experienced.

'Okay, but before we stop arguing I would like to point out that not going to university does not make someone ignorant or uneducated.'

'I've seen your résumé, remember? You had no educational qualifications. That makes you uneducated by anyone's standards but I listen to you and I can't square the circle. You went to one of the best schools in the world. Why no qualifications? Why have you only worked in hotels?'

This was what he wanted to talk about. The mystery of who Tabitha really was.

'My stepmother kicked me out on my eighteenth birthday and stopped paying the school fees.'

She said it so matter-of-factly that it took a moment for the implications of what she'd said to penetrate.

Giannis swore under his breath.

He'd considered calling Niki earlier for any recollections she might have of the teenage Tabitha but had concluded it would only make her query why he was asking and lead her to make assumptions. She'd already sent him a cheeky message:

Tabitha would make a great sister-in-law. Just saying!

Just saying? If he hadn't avoided responding to the message he would have teased her about her English slang usage.

He did not want to feed any speculation about their relationship until Tabitha consented to marry him.

He kept his eyes fixed on the road. 'Why did she do that?'

'Because she hates me,' she answered flatly before he felt the weight of her gaze fall on him. 'She's like your wife. She married my father for his money. The only saving grace I have is that he died not knowing what she was really like.'

His grip on the steering wheel tightened so much his knuckles turned white.

'What happened with her?'

Her silence was broken with a jaded laugh. 'Nothing.'

'She kicked you out for no reason?'

'She kicked me out so she could keep the inheritance for herself and her daughters.'

'*Your* inheritance?'

From the corner of his eye he saw her wipe her hair from her face. 'My father put his fortune in a trust. I don't know how things work in Greece but trusts are very common in England for those who want to preserve their wealth through the generations. The trust he had written was for the benefit of myself and Emmaline.'

'Emmaline's your stepmother?'

'Correct. Emmaline was also named as one of the trustees. The trustees control how the money is spent. My father's wishes were just that— wishes. Legally, I had to be supported by his estate and my education paid for until I turned eighteen. I turned eighteen during the first half-term break of my final school year. She was no longer obliged to pay the fees, so she didn't, and I didn't complete my secondary education.'

'Didn't the other trustees object?'

'There was only one other trustee. My father's best friend. Emmaline was sleeping with him. She had her claws in him as greatly as she'd had them in my father.'

Thinking her father must have been an incredibly weak man, but not voicing this private opinion, Giannis said, 'None of this sounds legal. Whether it was held in a trust or not, your father's wishes should have been carried out. Didn't you fight?'

'I couldn't.'

'Why not?' he asked incredulously. 'I'm certain any lawyer worth anything—'

'I had *nothing*,' Tabitha interrupted. A deep, itchy feeling had formed beneath her skin just to remember how helpless she had felt. 'When she threw me out she'd already packed a case for me. All I had was seventy pounds. It didn't cross my mind that I could fight her.'

'Why ever not?'

Hating the incredulity in his voice, she tried to explain. 'Because overnight my life became a matter of survival. Don't you understand that? I had nowhere to go and no one I could turn to for help. Both my parents were only children, all my grandparents were dead.'

'What about friends?'

'They were schoolgirls the same as me. What could they do? My closest friends weren't even English so I could hardly knock on their door and beg for help, could I?'

There was a long pause before he asked, in a softer tone, 'What did you do?'

'Hitched into Oxford and slept in a hostel for a couple of nights. It was the owners there who helped me find a live-in job at a small hotel in

Northamptonshire. The pay was awful but I had a bed to sleep in and they fed me too. Fighting back…?'

Hating the memories that were swarming out of her, Tabitha clasped the bag in her hands and twisted tightly. 'You have no idea what Emmaline is like. She puts on a façade that is so believable but beneath it she's rotten.'

'You are frightened of her?'

She had to swallow the dry lump in her throat before she could answer. These were things she had never spoken about. 'My father married her when I was ten. I was so excited and happy that I was going to have a new mummy and two sisters. I was desperate for siblings. They were older than me but really sweet to me. Emmaline was lovely to me too. It wasn't until after the marriage that their masks began to slip and I learned how rotten they were.'

'What did they do to you?'

'Lots of little cruel things. Fiona liked to hide pictures of clowns under my bedsheets. She knew I was scared of them. The first time she did it, I went running to my father and he scolded them. Fiona and Saffron both said sorry but then later that night they came into my room and woke me up. They stood either side of my bed and both pinched me hard on the underside of my arms. They said if I ever told on them again they would drown my cat. I believed them. I never told on them again.'

'They did more?'

'They couldn't touch me when I was at school—they went to a different one, thank goodness—but holidays were torture. They would bide their time and then when I was least expecting it do things like throw ink over my clothes or hide photos of horrible things like clowns and autopsies and stills from horror films in my drawers or bedsheets. Things that would either freak me out or get me into trouble.'

'And your father knew nothing of this?'

'I was too scared to tell him and I'd begun to be afraid of Emmaline. Her mask slipped too, but not as blatantly as her daughters'…nothing that anyone would notice. My father certainly didn't and there was nothing specific I could say to justify my feelings. It was more the way she looked at me when we were alone than anything. Like I was something unpleasant the cat had brought in. When he died there was no need for her to keep the façade up. The day after his funeral, she took down every photo of my mother and when I asked where they were she laughed.'

It still made her skin crawl to remember the coldness in that laughter. 'She still did her legal duty in feeding and clothing me but she acted like I was invisible. The times she did talk to me...' A shiver ran down her spine. 'She was like an ice sculpture that had come to life. She was cruel.'

'Why didn't you tell anyone?'

'And say what? And who could I have told? I was sixteen when my father died. I just kept telling myself all I had to do was work hard at school, get the grades I needed in my A Levels and then I could go to university and be free of her. I thought once I reached eighteen or went to university they would pay me enough of an allowance out of the trust that I wouldn't need to ever go back.'

'You wanted to leave your home to *her*?'

'I wanted to be *free* of her. I just assumed that one day she would die and I would be able to move back into my family home. I never thought for a minute she would go as far as to kick me out of it.' Hot, fat tears she'd been fighting back suddenly broke free and once they'd started she couldn't stop them.

Embarrassed at her weakness, she covered her face with her hands and pressed herself tightly against the window.

She'd never wanted to cry over her stepfamily's actions ever again but telling Giannis about it all had brought the pain back and made her realise how pathetic she had been.

Only when she felt a strong arm hook around her neck and haul her against his hard chest did she realise Giannis had pulled the car over. The unexpected comfort, and from Giannis of all people, only made her cry harder.

Giannis pressed his mouth into the cloud of hair beneath his chin and breathed deeply, trying hard to fight the rage swirling inside him that wanted to fly straight to England and destroy the woman who had destroyed Tabitha's life.

This Emmaline was as duplicitous as Anastasia had been but with added cruelty.

'She took everything,' Tabitha sobbed, her slender frame shaking in his arms, her tears soaking into his shirt. 'She took my home and my past and my future, and I let her.'

'You didn't.'

'I *did*. I never fought back because I was too scared. I never even went back to clear the rest of my bedroom. I told myself she would only have burned it all but the truth is I was too scared to face her, just like I was too scared to face you that morning. The truth is I'm a coward and I *hate* myself for that.'

Unwilling to listen to Tabitha castigate herself, he gently took her face in his hands and stared intently at her. 'Do not blame yourself for things that were out of your control, *koritzi mou*. What that woman did to you is despicable.'

And it would not go unavenged.

Her lips trembled, tears spilling over his fingers.

Hating to see her misery, he did what felt like the most natural thing in the world to give her comfort. He slipped his hands around to cradle the back of her neck and kissed her.

This kiss was nothing like the kisses they had devoured each other with before but a gentle, lingering brush of his lips to hers.

When he broke away her tears had stopped and she looked at him with an expression of bewilderment.

He pressed his forehead to hers and closed his

eyes, inhaling the wonderful fragrance that made every cell in his body come alive.

After long moments had passed he heard her take a deep inhalation before pulling away.

'Thank you,' she whispered.

'Parakalo.'

They sat in silence, no longer touching, until she said, 'Giannis…if we marry…'

His heart gave a sudden leap.

There was no longer bewilderment in the bloodshot eyes now staring at him as intently as he'd been staring at her.

'What are you thinking?'

'That if you do one thing for me, I will marry you.'

'What is that one thing?' He drew the line at setting a hitman on her stepmother. That would be too kind.

'I want you to write a will or contract that explicitly states that, if you die, everything you have goes to our child. It has to be cast-iron. Nothing ambiguous or open to interpretation. A cast-iron guarantee that, if anything happens to you, our child will be protected.'

'What about you?'

She gave a fierce shake of her head. 'I don't

want anything other than the right to be a mother to our child until he or she comes of age. If I die first then you will be the only parent. I know nothing is irreversible but—'

'I will get it done,' he interrupted, understanding why she was asking this of him. Her father had thought he'd protected his only child but it hadn't been enough to stop her stepmother taking everything. 'Our child will be named as my successor in my business and my sole heir.'

Her shoulders loosened and her head bowed. 'Thank you.'

Then their eyes met again and the spark that always flickered when he was with her flashed between them.

Knowing that now was the time to push aside the torrid emotions flowing through him, and harness the cool logic that had served him so well his whole adult life, Giannis turned the engine back on and pulled out of the spot where he'd carelessly parked.

'I will speak to my lawyer when we get home and get the wheels in motion,' he said conversationally. 'The documents will be drawn up and signed by the end of the week. We can marry next week. We will invite my family and leave it at that. Unless there is someone you would like to have there too?' He couldn't imagine who she would invite. She had no real family left.

There was a long pause before she sighed heavily and said, 'Actually…there is someone I would like to invite. My benefactor. Her name is Amelia Coulter and she's a live-in resident at your hotel.'

He had to concentrate hard to stop the car swerving off the road.

He'd forgotten all about Tabitha's mysterious benefactor, and it was the reason why he'd forgotten all about her existence that had him struggling to keep his concentration.

Without even realising it, he'd taken Tabitha at her word about her benefactor. He'd believed her without seeking proof as he always did.

Amelia Coulter was a name he'd become familiar with in his search for Tabitha, it having been on the guest list for his masquerade ball.

Keeping his voice as steady as he could manage, he said, 'She gave you her invitation?'

'She bought it for me.'

'Why?'

'As a thank you for taking care of her when she was sick.'

'That's an extravagant way to thank the hired help.'

He saw a slim shoulder rise in a shrug. 'There's sixty years between us but we'd become friends. She's mostly estranged from her family. They live in England. Her husband's buried in Vienna and she loves the city too much to want to leave it.'

'And what did you get from the friendship?' Only a day ago he would have added, 'Apart from a rich benefactor?' to his question but such cynicism would be wrong now.

'She reminds me of my grandmother.' There was a wistfulness to her voice and he found he didn't need her to explain any further.

Tabitha's life must have been lonely.

Giannis had never known loneliness. He'd always had his family, always had good friends, always been surrounded by people he could rely on. The only person who had ever let him down was the woman he had fallen in lust with and foolishly married. His humiliation at Anastasia's hands had been an unspoken secret within his circle but not one of them had taken the gossip to the press.

And now he was going to marry Tabitha, a

woman who elicited more desire in him than he'd known possible. A woman he felt the strangest compulsion to avenge. And protect.

He'd never wanted to protect anyone before. Not Anastasia, not even his sisters, who he'd always considered perfectly capable of protecting themselves.

These were all the feelings he'd sworn to avoid when he married again.

He'd had his head turned with lust before and had paid the price for it.

He had to get control of it all before it took control of him.

'I will arrange for an invitation to be given to her when we've set the date,' he said in a far more temperate voice than what lay beneath his skin. 'I will see the mayor tomorrow and get everything organised. He can marry us at my home.'

'Don't we have to marry in a church?'

He shuddered at the thought. 'No. We'll keep it a small affair. I've done the big, white wedding. I have no wish to go through that again.'

Her ensuing silence sat uncomfortably in his guts.

CHAPTER NINE

THE FOLLOWING WEEK sped by. Tabitha signed more documents and read through more paperwork in that time than she'd done in her entire life. She'd been taken aback at the speed with which Giannis had got things done but barely had time to blink let alone think. Which was probably just as well. She had a big enough headache as it was without adding thinking to the list.

And now their wedding was only one day away.

For the first time since Tabitha had agreed to marry him, Giannis had left the villa without her. He'd flown to Athens and would be spending the evening in his apartment there, the one traditional part of a wedding he intended to embrace.

Was that because he wanted a breather from her? Or because he genuinely feared it would bring bad luck to their marriage if they saw each other the night before the wedding?

Until that morning, she had spent all her waking time with him. He'd included her in everything: lawyers' meetings and the visit to his family to break the good news about their wedding. He'd flown her to England so they could get her birth certificate and had visited the embassy. He'd taken her to Athens for a day shopping for clothes, insisting on buying every single item that caught her eye, even those on which she had done nothing more than brush her fingers. As a result she had a wardrobe stuffed with beautiful, expensive clothes, which she had no chance of wearing all of before she became too big with child to fit in them, and a dressing table crammed with more cosmetics than a professional make-up artist possessed and more perfumes than a perfumer could sniff in a career.

When she had protested at this unnecessary extravagance, she'd been rebuffed with a, 'You are going to be a Basinas. When it is time for you to wear maternity clothes, we will go shopping again.'

She should be grateful for this time away from him, should be making the most of her last few hours of freedom, not moping around as if she missed him.

But she found she was missing him. The gregarious man she had fallen into a romantic dream with the night of the ball was slowly emerging from the austere shell into which the truth of her identity had put him.

She found she had to keep reminding herself that their marriage was not about them. It was all for their baby. She was not his wife of choice and now she feared he no longer even desired her.

He hadn't laid a finger on her since that small, comforting kiss in his car.

There had been more occasions than she could count when she had found herself trapped in the heat of his gaze but he'd made no move. What was stopping him from touching her?

And what was stopping her from touching him? She *ached* to touch him but something kept holding her back.

To keep the demons in her head from plaguing her too much, she decided to tidy her bedroom and clean her bathroom. Tomorrow they would no longer be hers. She would be in Giannis's bed, a thought that made her scrub the shower door that little bit harder.

'What are you doing?'

She whipped round to find Giannis at the bathroom doorway, a bemused expression on his face.

'What are you doing here?' she asked dumbly.

The ghost of a smile appeared on his lips then disappeared as a furrow cleaved his forehead. 'I'll answer that once you've answered my question. Why are you cleaning? I pay staff to clean.'

'I needed to do something.'

Now his brow rose quizzically. 'Did it have to involve cleaning bathrooms?'

'No, I cleaned my room too,' she answered tartly, desperate to cover the mortification soaking her. Who wanted to be caught scrubbing a shower dressed in a pair of designer denim shorts and a designer short-sleeved shirt she'd tied around her midriff, clothing he'd spent a small fortune on?

Taking a softer tone, she added, 'Cleaning's therapeutic and, let's be honest, something I'm good at.'

He nodded slowly, his expression softening too. 'We will have to think of something else for you to do when you're in need of something therapeutic to do, or Zoe will be worried for her job, but that is something for us to think about after the wedding. The reason I'm here is because I have a gift for you.'

From behind his back he produced a small box, the logo on it signalling that it contained a smart phone.

'I've already set it up for you,' he said while she examined it, hands shaking at his unexpected appearance.

He'd flown back just to give her a phone?

'It's the latest model,' he continued. 'I've programmed my number into it and downloaded an app that acts as a translator. It means you'll be able to converse with Zoe and anyone else without a language barrier.'

'How does it work?'

She put the phone into his open hand and sat next to him on the sofa. She didn't even remember walking from the bathroom to the bedroom with him.

Eyes alight with curiosity, she watched him press an icon. The screen lit up and he brought it to his mouth and said something in Greek. A moment later a disembodied voice rang out, 'Your hair needs a brush.'

She gave a shout of laughter and met clear blue eyes gleaming with an amusement she hadn't seen since the ball. It was a gleam that made her heart leap and suddenly she was aware that they were sat closer together than they had been in the past week. For all the time they'd spent together, this was the first time they'd been within touching distance of each other when alone.

The gleam in his eyes as they stared at each other slowly dimmed, the amusement on his lips fading. Tabitha's own lips began to tingle, the nerves on her skin firing, anticipation lacing through her as their faces tilted and closed in...

But then Giannis pulled back, cleared his throat and, without missing a beat, without any hint that he'd just been about to kiss her, murmured, 'Now you say something into it. It's programmed to translate both our languages.'

Blinking rapidly, trying to pretend that what had nearly happened just then hadn't, she took the phone back and brought it up to her chin. Striving for the same lightness he'd displayed when speaking into it, she said, 'You need a shave.'

Again, barely a moment passed before the same disembodied voice rang out, this time in Greek.

Tabitha put the phone onto her lap and stared

at it, suddenly aware that hot tears were burning the back of her eyes and desperate not to let them fall.

This phone, although a drop in the ocean for a man of Giannis's wealth, was the most thoughtful gift he could have given her. It stopped her being isolated when she didn't have him there to translate.

'Thank you,' she whispered when she was reasonably confident she could speak without blubbing. Who cried over a *phone*? How ridiculous! The pregnancy hormones must be getting stronger.

Hormones or not, she had to start tempering the wild feelings Giannis evoked in her. Being with him heightened every normal emotion. He could turn her from joy to despondency and twist it all back again in the time it took to switch on a light. One look and her body's responses took a life of their own, her entire being practically salivating for him.

How could she contain it, she thought with despair, especially now that he'd stopped treating her like the Antichrist? Little acts of kindness had the capacity to melt her heart in the same way one little look from him melted her bones.

Combine the two and she became a puddle of mush for him.

'It is my pleasure.' He took the phone from her lap without touching her skin and continued in the same nonchalant tone. 'It's retina-activated like my own phone. Once it's done, only you will be able to access it.'

Minutes later and it was all set up and Tabitha was trying hard to concentrate on some of the other features Giannis was showing her. He said something about a music app but his words had become distant, a direct effect of his body having inched closer to hers, her senses catching whiffs of the spicy scent she'd become greedy for.

He swiped the screen at the same moment his thigh pressed against hers.

Tabitha gritted her teeth and tried her hardest to ignore the fresh heat careering through her.

But then he put his hand on her thigh.

Holding her breath, she stared down at the long, tanned fingers resting on her bare flesh…

'What kind of music do you like to listen to?' Giannis repeated, wondering why Tabitha had suddenly become mute. 'You can put in bands and genres and it will select…'

And then he followed her gaze and realised his

hand was on her thigh, his middle finger making little circles over the silky skin.

For a moment all he could do was stare at it dumbly before cursing himself.

Would his weakness for this woman ever be controlled?

Being with Tabitha meant being in a constant state of arousal, a condition he'd spent the past week controlling. It had been an internal battle he'd been determined to win, a battle to prove to himself that he could master his reactions around her, a battle he'd thought he was winning.

For the first time since she'd agreed to marry him, he'd unintentionally dropped his guard and now his hand was resting on her thigh as if it were the most natural gesture in the world.

He inhaled deeply to counteract the thuds of his suddenly heavy heartbeats and moved his hand away without comment.

He'd made a vow to himself not to touch Tabitha again until their wedding night, thinking he would have mastered his reactions to her enough by then that when they did make love, it would be an enjoyable experience but not in the world-shifting way it had been on their one full night together.

'We've had a package couriered over,' he said into the electrified silence, his voice sounding thick to his ears. 'Your Mrs Coulter sent it. A wedding gift.'

'That's sweet of her,' Tabitha whispered, her own voice containing the faintest hint of a tremor.

Mrs Coulter had regretfully declined the invitation to their wedding, not feeling physically strong enough to make the journey over. To make up for Tabitha's disappointment, Giannis had suggested she fly to Vienna with him for his next monthly trip to his hotel.

He opened his mouth to remind her of this but the words fell away from his tongue when he met cornflower eyes wide and stark on his.

The groan escaped from his throat before he could hold it back, turning into a growl when his hands cupped the cheeks heightened with colour.

He could control this...

He brought his mouth down to capture the beautiful heart-shaped lips in one long, hot, wet, devouring kiss.

His loins sang their delight but he mastered his reactions with a ruthlessness that would have made a Tibetan monk proud. Breaking the kiss, he captured her chin, and this time allowed himself to stare deep into eyes pulsing their own desire back at him, the fingers of his other hand twisting the long, silky locks of her hair.

A sudden wave of possessiveness crashed through him along with an overwhelming urge to gather her into his arms, carry her to the bed and make her his in every way possible.

'Tomorrow night, *matia mou*, you will be my wife and in my bed. Until then…' He pressed one more, lighter kiss to her lips, breathing in her scent for good measure. It infused him, sinking deep into his veins…

He got abruptly to his feet.

He'd played with the flame of Tabitha's fire enough. A man had his limits and the burning ache in his loins proved he'd reached his.

'I will see you on the sun terrace tomorrow. Enjoy getting acquainted with your new toy.'

Tabitha watched him leave with her hand pressed tightly to her chest, her heart hammering against her palm.

Her blood pumped thick and strong inside her veins, as it did every time he kissed or touched her, her skin alive in a way that was becoming familiar to her but there had been none of the rightness she'd felt since their very first dance.

Giannis had flown back from Athens especially to give her the phone.

He was doing everything he could to make her transition into his life as easy as it could be.

Their wedding night promised so much…

So why did she feel so wretched?

The answer to Tabitha's wretchedness came to her three hours before they exchanged their vows.

She'd eaten a light, plain lunch alone on the pool terrace and then, limbs heavy, had gone to her bedroom to get ready for the wedding.

Two members of staff were in there, moving the last of her new wardrobe and accessories to the marital bedroom she would from that night share with Giannis.

It was the bedroom Anastasia must have shared with him.

Anastasia's ghost was the cause of her wretchedness, she realised with a strong churn of nausea.

Every step Tabitha took in this magnificent villa had been taken by the woman before her.

Giannis might desire her but he would never feel for Tabitha what he'd felt for his first wife.

It shredded her insides to know she was being denied a proper wedding because he'd already shared one with Anastasia.

She remembered that wedding picture of the two of them. It was one of dozens to be found on the Internet. Giannis and Anastasia's wedding had been a humungous affair with guests including the cream of Hollywood and European royalty. It had been a true celebration of their love.

For Tabitha's wedding, the only people he was inviting were his immediate family. No cousins or aunts and uncles. No friends. Their wedding was no celebration.

It shredded her insides even more to know she shouldn't care if they had what she considered to be a proper wedding or not. She shouldn't care that she would exchange her vows on Giannis's sun terrace and not in one of the beautiful, blue-topped white churches Santorini was famous for, and that she would be wearing a simple white summer dress instead of the big, flouncy traditional dress she'd dreamed of wearing when she'd been young and dreams had still existed within her.

She shouldn't care that Giannis didn't love her and would never love her.

It might have ended horrendously but he'd already had a marriage for love. With Anastasia.

She didn't want his love, she told herself with a stubborn desperation. She was marrying him to protect her unborn child's future, the exact same reason he was marrying her, and her irrational jealousy towards his first wife was…well, irrational. More than irrational. Heinous. Anastasia was dead, her life extinguished before she'd reached the age of thirty. What kind of monster was Tabitha to feel jealous of a ghost?

Emotions threatening to suffocate her, she opened one of the bedroom windows but was met with blazing heat.

She needed to get ready! She was hours away from marrying Giannis and all she could do was pace her bedroom, working herself into a lather.

If only she had someone with her, she thought despairingly, wishing her father could be there. She remembered him telling her as a child never to settle for second best, that she was worthy of only the greatest man to marry.

She wasn't settling for second best. Giannis was. He desired her. She thought he might even be coming to like her. But she was the woman with whom he'd had a one-night stand and he was marrying her from the consequence of that one night so he could claim their child as his own.

Her father would have loved Giannis, not for his mega-wealth and rumoured royal connections, but for his strong family bonds. Those were the kinds of bonds he'd been eager to create for Tabitha when he'd married Emmaline.

If her father had been alive she would have put her foot down and insisted on a big, white wedding but without him there, without any guests of her own, how could she complain? She wasn't contributing anything to their marriage financially or otherwise.

But how she wished Giannis thought enough of her that he would want to recite their vows in a sacred, sanctified building and give her the dream of her childhood.

Feeling herself on the verge of crying, she sucked the unshed tears back in at the loud rap on her door.

Thinking it must be the staff returning to collect more of her stuff, she opened it and found her heart lightening to see Niki there, arms laden with flowers, beaming widely. 'Hello, future sister-in-law. I've appointed myself your maid of honour, hairdresser and make-up artist. It's time to turn you into a beautiful bride.'

Giannis stood on his sun terrace, adorned with cascades of flowers and balloons, courtesy of his sisters, and closed his eyes at the warmth of the late-afternoon sun on his face.

Anyone looking at him would assume he was a man at complete ease with the vows he was about to exchange.

They would not see the tight knots coiling in his guts that were at odds with what felt suspiciously like butterflies in his stomach.

He could not remember the last time he'd felt so...nervous?

He pushed that irrational thought away. What was there to be nervous about? Whatever happened in this marriage, his fortune was protected. Tabitha would be provided for in the event of divorce or his death but he had taken her at her word and made his will, their pre-nuptial agreement and the contract he'd had drawn up for the business iron-tight. His child and any other children they might have would receive everything.

His phone buzzed in his pocket and he pulled it out to read the email from his private investigator. It was an update on the investigations Giannis had instructed be done on Emmaline Brigstock and Tabitha.

He experienced the now familiar twinge of guilt about having Tabitha investigated too, although the investigation of her was very much secondary to her stepmother. He was being prudent. He'd been bitten badly before and would not be fooled again. If there were skeletons in Tabitha's closet she had failed to tell him about, or discrepancies in her version of events of her past, he would learn them.

Tabitha had enchanted him from the first moment he'd set eyes on her. She had more power than she could ever know but he would not allow the spell she wove around him to entangle him any tighter than it had ensnared him before.

He sent a quick response, reiterating his desire for thoroughness over speed, and had just put his phone back in his pocket when the sound of loud chatter filled the air.

His family had arrived.

He greeted them warmly, sharing embraces and kisses with his parents, three of his four sisters, his three brothers-in-law and his handful of noisy small nieces and nephews.

As much as he would have preferred a wedding with only the two of them, his family would have been outraged to miss it. Tabitha was joining their family. She would become one of them. It was only right they be there to witness the union. And there was not a single member of his family who didn't love a good party.

There had been a complete lack of surprise when he'd introduced Tabitha to his family as his fiancée. Tabitha had been as white as a sheet but they'd welcomed her as if they'd known her for years. In Niki's case, she had. Her obvious bout of gossiping about his and Tabitha's relationship had eased the path to acceptance. Tabitha came from a good family, was well-educated, beautiful, shy but friendly and already had Niki's affection. That she was already carrying Giannis's child was simply the icing on the cake.

His youngest sister had been the only one annoyed that he wasn't having a traditional wedding. She'd pulled him aside to demand answers, which he had brushed off, using the same excuse he had with Tabitha—that he'd done the big, white wedding and saw no need for another.

'And is Tabitha happy to be denied her own white wedding?' she'd asked shrewdly.

'She is in agreement with me.'

His sister had snorted in reply but wisely let the matter go.

He'd been the one unable to let it go. Until Niki had asked him the question it had never occurred to him that Tabitha hadn't responded to his declaration that theirs would be a simple wedding.

As his family parted to take their seats and their chatter turned to hush, indicating that his bride was making her way up the pebbled steps to join them, Giannis reminded himself yet again that the only reason either of them was taking this step was for their child.

And then she appeared, Niki at her side beaming from ear to ear.

The ballooning of his heart pushed the air from his lungs.

Suddenly he was transported back to the night of the ball when he'd first glimpsed Tabitha on the stairs, when his pulses had raced and he'd been unable to tear his eyes from her.

Her beauty that night had dazzled him.

He'd wondered the next morning if she could be the one his family had urged him to find. He'd never had the chance to find out because she'd vanished. So much had happened since that early morning that he'd forgotten the question had played in his head.

Her eyes found his. A small, shy smile curved on her cheeks.

His heart stopped. It shuddered. It kick-started back to life.

The white cotton dress she wore was long and flowing and would look as at home on a beach as it did for this simple ceremony. On her feet were flat Roman-style sandals. Her long hair hung in loose curls around her shoulders and down her back. Her small hands, the once functionally short nails now elegant and polished, clutched a posy of flowers.

When she reached his side the mayor who was officiating the ceremony cleared his throat.

The vows they exchanged were as simple as the ceremony itself and, as Tabitha recited hers, cornflower-blue eyes never leaving his, Giannis's throat closed as the truth hit him.

Tabitha deserved better than this.

She wanted nothing for herself other than the right to be a mother to her own child. She could have demanded anything and everything but her only thought was for their child to have the love of both parents. It was for love of their unborn child that she was committing her life to his.

She deserved more than this simple exchange of vows on the roof of his home, even if the location and views were as stunning as anywhere else on his island.

When it was his turn to recite his own vows, he gazed deeply into her eyes and made a silent vow to himself to be the husband she deserved.

He would never love her but he would give his last breath to protect her.

Tabitha had magic in her veins. When he kissed her to seal the vows they'd exchanged, he felt its power seep through his lips and into his bloodstream.

CHAPTER TEN

TABITHA HADN'T HAD a drop of the champagne the rest of the Basinases had consumed in vast quantities but she felt as drunk as if she'd downed a whole magnum of it.

The vows they'd exchanged...

Somehow they'd contained far more meaning than she'd expected.

In truth, she'd expected the ceremony to feel like a farce but it hadn't. She'd meant every word she'd said and, from the look in Giannis's eyes when he'd spoken his vows, he'd meant it too.

Afterwards, they stayed on the terrace and shared a feast with his family.

Her family.

They didn't say it in words but they didn't need to. The Basinas family accepted her as one of their own. Their acceptance filled her heart to the brim.

For hours they talked, laughed, ate and drank. Toasts were made, blessings given for their marriage and the safe delivery of their child and childhood escapades revealed, all the while Giannis's small nieces and nephews ran around chasing each other and playing pranks on any family member they could.

This was the family life Tabitha had dreamed of when she'd been a child, the family life her father had wanted for her. When the full moon rose high in the night sky she looked up at it and wondered if he was up there too, looking down at her. If he was, she knew he would have a smile the size of that moon on his face.

But it wasn't just his family. It was Giannis too. She hadn't seen him so at ease since the night of the ball, not just with his family but with her too. Every time she looked at him his eyes would pulse and a knowing smile tug at his lips.

Anticipation laced her veins but there was dread mingled with it too.

For all the unexpected joy she'd found in their ceremony and small celebration, she just could not shift the image of Anastasia from her head.

How could she share Giannis's bed knowing he'd shared it with the love of his life before her?

Eventually it was time to call it a night. The small children were rounded up, all protesting wildly that they didn't want to go home, that they weren't tired, even while their little faces stretched with the yawns they couldn't fight.

And then the front door closed and they were alone.

After all that boisterous noise the silence was stark.

She gazed at her husband, the only sound her rapidly accelerating heartbeats.

He locked the door then slowly stepped towards her. 'You enjoyed yourself?'

'Very much.' She attempted a smile. 'I never knew you were such a troublemaker as a child.' His sisters had recounted many of his escapades with glee.

He stood before her and caught a lock of her hair in his hands. 'Did I ever tell you why I hosted the ball?'

'Wasn't it to find a wife?'

He brought the lock to his face and inhaled. Shivers cascaded up her spine. 'That was part of it. The ball itself came about because of a debt owed from my school days. When I was fifteen I broke into the headmaster's office and superglued all his furniture to the floor and all his stationery and books to his desk and shelves.'

'Why?' she whispered in fascination.

'One of the other boys dared me to. In those days I could never resist a challenge. The headmaster knew it was me but couldn't prove it. I was on my final warning. If Alessio hadn't given me an alibi, I would have been expelled.'

'You hosted a ball as repayment for an alibi twenty years ago?'

'A man must always pay his debts, *matia mou*. Without that alibi, my life might have taken a very different path.'

Giannis had always been a risk-taker. Being the only boy of five children probably had something to do with it. His sisters had always been good. Apart from Niki but, seeing as she'd looked up to him as her role model, that probably explained her own mischievous behaviour.

He'd delighted in driving his sisters to distraction, especially Katarina, the only one older than him and thus the bossiest, by climbing the tallest trees and buildings, stealing the gardener's ride-on mower for illicit joyrides, and then progressing to their father's car and stealing cigarettes, defiantly smoking them one after the other until he'd made himself sick. Anything they said he shouldn't do, he'd made it his business to do.

That had included marrying Anastasia, he now realised.

His sisters had all hated her on sight. They had never said it in words but the Basinases were a close-knit bunch and he'd been able to read his sisters' feelings all too well.

Their disapproval had only added to Anastasia's allure.

Skimming his fingers down the swan of Tabitha's elegant neck, revelling in the way her lips parted and her breathing shallowed, he ruefully considered what his reaction would have been if they'd disapproved of her.

Tabitha had an unidentifiable *something* that was far greater than mere allure, something that sang to all his senses, a conductor tuning them into harmony. The desire ringing from the cornflower eyes was more intoxicating than the strongest of spirits.

She could have no greater appeal. Not to him.

It was not humanly possible for him to desire her more than he did.

The past week spent attempting to master that desire had been torturous but, he felt sure, successful.

The spell she wove on him was nothing but an illusion and now he would prove it.

He would make love to her and when it was over the earth would still be on its axis.

Trailing his fingers down her arm, he took her hand in his and tugged it gently. 'Time for us to go to bed, Kyría Basinas.'

Fingers entwined, they climbed the stairs in silence to the room that now belonged to them both, sexual chemistry thick in the air surrounding them.

But, when they reached the door, she hesitated at the threshold.

He brought her hand to his lips and stared into the eyes brimming with uncertainty. 'Is something the matter, *matia mou*?'

She stilled, teeth sinking into her bottom lip, her stare now filled with something he didn't recognise. 'Did you share this room with Anastasia?'

Taken aback at both the question and her first ever mention of his dead wife, it took a few seconds for him to realise why she was asking it.

'Anastasia hated Santorini. She loved the city life. She didn't spend one night here. No woman has shared this bed with me.'

While it sank in that Tabitha had insecurities about his first wife, and what the implications of that could mean, something happened that distracted his thoughts entirely.

Right before his eyes, Tabitha grew in stature and a light came into her eyes that didn't just shine from them but infused the whole of her in a warm glow.

Before he could register the change, she put a hand to his chest then stepped forward and rested her cheek on it and breathed deeply.

She was inhaling his scent…

Then she tipped her head back and gave him a smile of such knowing radiance, every cell in his body tightened.

Gently she pushed him across the threshold and kicked the door shut behind them with her heel. And then she slid her arms around his neck and pulled his head down so she could kiss him.

Heat licked through his veins, his physical awareness—always there, always a part of him around her—flickering at the first brush of her lips to his. When her tongue darted into his mouth and she pressed herself tightly against him, the flickering turned to full arousal.

Hunger exploded in him and he wrapped his

arms tightly around her. His hands delved into the silky tresses, fingers coiling in it as he devoured her...and she devoured him.

Tabitha was the one to steer them to the bed, to push him onto it, the one to break the kiss, to run her lips over his cheeks and down his neck as he had done to her, scorching his flesh with every mark from her mouth and tongue. It was her fingers that worked their way down the buttons of his shirt and then pushed it apart, pulled it down his arms and threw it onto the floor. It was her hands pushing at his chest until he was laid flat on his back, breathing deeply, wondering where this vixen had suddenly appeared from.

She put her mouth to his ear and bit the lobe gently. 'Don't move,' she whispered before reaching out an arm to turn on his bedside light.

He had no intention of moving anywhere.

Giannis had anticipated this night in detail, over and over, imagining her breasts in his mouth, his fingers caressing her, inside her, his mouth tasting her, exploring every inch of her so thoroughly that every part of her was as familiar as his own reflection was to him.

But never had he anticipated that she would be the one making the moves. Taking control.

Every inch of his body throbbed with anticipation, heat thick through his loins and veins.

She jumped off the bed with all the grace of a dancer, bounded to the main light switch by the door and hit it. Immediately the light in the room went from full illumination to dusky, casting them both in shadow.

Tabitha stared at the man she'd committed her life to, drinking in his devilish beauty, then bent over to remove her sandals. When they were off, she pinched the skirt of her dress in her fingers and brought it up and over her head.

The suck of air he took only added to the heady thrills zipping through her veins.

Their wedding might not have been the one of her dreams but she felt as if she'd slipped into another Giannis-filled dream. The relief at being told no other woman had shared this room with him had been dizzying, unleashing an enormous wave of emotion she could never find the words to explain. That wave had filled her entirely and suddenly she had found herself emboldened to act on her desires, and emboldened to express in a language they both understood everything she felt for him in that moment.

She wanted him, this beautiful Greek man who

could sear her skin with nothing more than a look. She wanted him so much that there were times she could hardly breathe for her longing.

Hooking her arms behind her to undo her lacy bra, she pulled the straps down her arms and threw it onto her discarded dress.

The seductive appreciation in his hooded eyes sent arrows of bittersweet longing shooting from her breasts to her pelvis and gave her the courage needed to remove the last item of clothing and stand before him naked.

Giannis swallowed. His greedy eyes devoured every detail.

The incredible womanly body he'd relived every inch of every night since they'd conceived their child was there before him. The differences the pregnancy was making were there too, subtle but to his eyes obvious.

They only made her more beautiful.

The full breasts were larger, the hips a little wider...the stomach a little rounder.

He wanted to tell her how beautiful she was but his throat had closed.

He couldn't speak.

He didn't need to.

She must have read his thoughts for she smiled

then walked slowly back to the bed, climbed onto it and straddled him.

Impossibly, his arousal grew, the ache in it a pain he was unable to relieve.

Gazing down at him, she placed her hands on his chest and let her fingers drift over it.

He reached out an arm to touch her silky skin but she stopped him and shook her head. 'Not yet,' she whispered.

And then she leaned forward and kissed him deeply. Her breasts brushed lightly against his chest, a tease of sensation he craved so much more of. When he tried to wrap his arms around her she shrugged him off and nipped his bottom lip. 'Not *yet*,' she repeated sternly.

She bestowed him with one more kiss on his mouth and then her lips trailed down his neck again. But this time she didn't stop.

This time she continued her oral exploration, tongue and mouth kissing and licking every inch of his chest, his nipples, down to his abdomen, her fingers working on his trousers, which she pulled down with his underwear and threw unceremoniously onto the floor.

This time she was the one to feast her eyes on

him, lashes sweeping, a look of wonder on her face as she gazed at his jutting erection.

She put a hand to it.

He gritted his teeth as it throbbed at her touch.

And then she leant down to cover it with her mouth.

A loud, unbidden groan escaped his throat and he had to fist the sheets and grit his teeth even tighter to fight back the orgasm already threatening release.

'Tabitha...'

He could speak no more.

All he was capable of doing was raising his head to gaze dazedly down at the honey-blonde hair over his lap and submit to the pleasure she was giving him.

It was possibly the clumsiest but most incredible experience of his life.

He'd never known sensation like it.

She was doing this because she wanted to give *him* pleasure.

From the soft sounds she was making, she was enjoying it too.

The tension he fought against releasing was building inside him, every part of him thick with it, enveloping the whole of his body, the conductor of his senses harmonising them to a perfect pitch.

Suddenly he could take no more.

He wanted to come. Badly. More than he'd ever needed to come before. But he wanted to be inside her and watch as she came too.

He gathered her hair in his hands and gently raised her head. 'Come here,' he commanded thickly.

Eyes dark with desire met his and then her hands were patting over his chest as she moved gracefully back up to straddle him again. But this time she positioned herself exactly where he ached for her to be.

Her lips found his mouth at the same moment she sank fully onto him, taking him whole inside her hot, wet heat.

His groan came from deep within him.

Theos...

Giannis screwed his eyes closed and fought back the release his tortured body burned for.

She'd stilled. Her pubis was ground against him, his erection fully sheathed inside her, but she made no effort to move.

He took a deep breath and opened his eyes.

The expression on her face almost made him come there and then.

Cupping her cheeks with his hands, he gazed at the flushed face in wonderment. 'Do whatever you want, *matia mou.*'

Her eyes closed briefly and then she carefully raised herself back so her hands rested on his chest and she was gazing down at him with that heady, glazed look.

'That's it,' he urged. 'You set the pace.'

She rode him slowly to start with, her fingers digging into his chest, lips parted, eyes fixed on his face, adjusting her position until she found the one that had her moaning and her movements increasing.

It was the most erotic experience he had ever known.

Holding her hip with one hand to steady her, he reached his other up and cupped one of the breasts swaying so gently.

Her breathing deepened.

He brushed a thumb over the tip and watched her eyes widen and dilate in response, taking as much enjoyment and pleasure from watching Tabitha's expressive face as he did from the incredible sensations raging through him.

How he held on, he didn't know. It was an elemental torture he'd never known existed, pleasure and pain entwined together, and when she threw her head back with a cry and ground down on him one final time, the tight thickening pulled him as deep inside her as it was possible to go and pushed him over the edge.

His orgasm burst through him with a force that had him shouting out her name, pulsations of indescribable pleasure crashing through every part of him.

Tabitha, her face burrowed in Giannis's neck, his arms wrapped tightly around her, slowly came floating back down to earth.

She could feel the beat of his heart on her breasts crushed against his chest. She could hear the deep raggedness of his breaths.

He was still inside her.

She didn't want to move.

She didn't want to break the spell.

His arms loosened as his fingers wound through her hair.

'Where the hell did that come from?' he asked with a choked laugh.

She nuzzled into his neck and gave a short giggle. 'I have no idea.'

But of course she knew. It had been a release from her fears of the ghost of Anastasia, something for just Tabitha and Giannis, an embrace of the start of the rest of their lives together.

She wanted to hold on to this closeness she felt at that exact moment and bottle it for ever.

She felt so much. Too much, she feared, although it was a thought to be dealt with another time, when she wasn't still feeling the thrills of their love-making vibrate through her skin.

Moving her face from the heaven that was the crook of Giannis's neck, she rested her chin on his chest. 'We can have a good marriage, can't we?' she asked in a small voice.

He was silent for a moment before he shifted from beneath her and rolled her over so he was the one lying on top of her.

His face hovered over hers, his hands smoothing her hair from her forehead.

He kissed the tip of her nose.

'I meant my vows,' he said seriously.

'So did I,' she whispered.

'I know you did. There has been much distrust between us and many misconceptions but we can make this marriage work. If we use our vows and the rings we wear on our fingers as lines in the sand, we can put the doubts and distrust behind us.'

Warmth filled her heart. With a soft sigh she put her hand on the nape of his neck and gazed into the eyes staring at her with such sincerity. 'I want to make it work.'

His lips brushed against hers. 'You already are.'

CHAPTER ELEVEN

THE SUN POURING into the bedroom woke Tabitha from the deep slumber she'd finally fallen into.

Giannis's side empty, she stretched and climbed out, looking for something to wear. She settled on the shirt she'd practically ripped from his body, still discarded on the floor where she'd thrown it.

A powerful sense of *déjà vu* hit her but she was too full of bliss from a night spent making exquisite love to fear the irony that the last time she'd spent the night with him she'd also woken to an empty bed and helped herself to his shirt.

They were married now. She carried his child in her belly.

For the first time since she'd been ten years old, Tabitha woke without a single fear in her mind.

It was liberating.

As she fastened the buttons of the shirt that fell to her knees, she gazed around at Giannis's bedroom. *Their* bedroom.

It was like a whitewashed cave with curved ceilings, thick arches and an abundance of alcoves, some covered with doors, others with seats carved into them or modern artwork placed in them.

She found a bathroom that thrilled her feminine heart, a dressing room filled with Giannis's clothes, another dressing room filled with *her* clothes... She quickly shut that door so she didn't have to change out of his shirt.

Padding to the other side of the room to one of the huge arched windows, she was astounded to find a private balcony with an infinity pool and immediately set about locating the door to it.

She found it behind the silk drapes hanging at the far end of the room and stepped out onto it. The sun's rays were already strong that morning, the cloudless sky a deep royal-blue.

'I was afraid for a moment that you'd done another early-morning vanishing act.' Giannis's deep, rich voice rumbled deliciously through her ears and she turned with a smile to face him.

He wore only a pair of shorts and carried a tray with coffee, orange juice and a variety of pastries and fruits.

He grinned, placing the tray on the glass table

by the thick-walled balustrade. 'But I see you have stolen another of my shirts.'

As her heart had lodged into her throat at the first sight of him, it took a few moments before speech came. 'You wasted all that money on clothes for me when you could have just given me your discarded shirts.'

'If you wore only my shirts neither of us would ever leave my room.' And then he pulled her to him and kissed her so thoroughly, her knees weakened. 'Good morning, *matia mou.*'

Staring into the gleaming eyes, she smiled again. She couldn't stop smiling. 'Good morning.'

Anticipating another kiss, she was disappointed when he let her go and pulled a chair out for her. 'Sit. Eat.'

She raised a brow at his authoritative tone.

He winked and took his seat. 'I find I have a great appetite this morning.'

Laughing, she sat and helped herself to a glass of orange juice.

She could hardly credit that only twenty-four hours ago she'd been filled with dread. Now she felt as light as air, as if she could fly.

Giannis gazed in wonder at the radiance shining from his new wife, his relief at finding her still there now tamed.

While he'd waited for the coffee to brew he'd had an unexpected feeling of *déjà vu* flash through him.

The last time he'd made her coffee after a night of making love, he'd returned to an empty room.

This time the room had been empty but she had still been there.

The smile she had greeted him with could have melted an iceberg.

The night they had shared...

Theos, his loins still thrummed from the effects.

Biting into an apple, he chewed and swallowed the bite before saying, 'We have the next three days to ourselves. Is there anything you would like to do?'

She pulled a face as she considered the question. 'Can we stay in bed?'

'You read my mind.'

Their eyes met. His heart thumped hard against his ribs.

That was to be expected. After the night they'd shared, all of him felt out of kilter. Three days of making love to his beautiful bride would be enough for everything to right itself.

She broke into a bread roll and spooned honey on it. 'What happens after the three days are up? Are you going back to work?'

'I have to,' he answered regretfully. 'And I might have to answer the occasional urgent email while we're here. I have many business interests and, while I employ the best people to run them for me, any issues are ultimately my responsibility.'

She bit into the roll and shrugged, clearly conveying that she understood.

'What did you want to do?' he asked curiously.

She looked at him with a frown, her mouth still full of food.

'Before Emmaline kicked you out of your home and cut your education off. What did you hope to do? Would you have gone to university?'

She swallowed her mouthful and took another drink of orange juice. 'I wanted to do a business degree.'

He raised a brow in admiration. 'What would you have done with it?'

'The plan was for me to take over my father's business.'

'What business was he in?'

'He owned a brewery.'

Recognition flashed through him. 'Brigstock Brewery? That's your family's business?'

He remembered it well. His first illicit pint of beer at boarding school had been in one of its pubs.

'It's been in the family for over two hundred years,' she said with a touch of pride. 'We own over two thousand pubs and restaurants and brew many of our own beers.'

'Who runs it now?'

She gave a shrug but he caught the sadness in her eyes. 'It's not been family-run since my mother died. My father gave up day-to-day control of it so he could look after me. It's run by a board of directors but he was still the majority shareholder. He'd started easing back into the business a couple of years before he died. The plan was always for me to one day take my place on the board too.'

It was an answer that led to so many further questions, he hardly knew where to start. 'How old were you when your mother died?'

'Four. She died of cervical cancer. My father died when I was sixteen, of a heart attack. Probably the stress of being married to Emmaline,' she added with a bitter murmur.

'If he was the majority shareholder then presumably he was entitled to a majority share of the profits?'

Her eyes met his. There was a stoniness in them he'd seen only once before. 'Those profits go into the trust.'

He felt his own blood turn stony. 'Meaning they go to Emmaline?'

She nodded.

He drummed his fingers on the table, thinking hard, biting back irrational heated thoughts of hitmen and torture. 'You need to fight this.'

'I wouldn't know where to begin.'

'You begin at the start. With Emmaline. She has taken—'

'I know what she's taken and done,' she interrupted with a hint of anger. 'I've lived with the consequences for almost five years.'

'You don't have to live with them any more. Let me help you. We can take back what was yours.'

'No!' Tabitha's shout of disagreement surprised her as much as it clearly surprised him. Lowering her voice, she said evenly, 'The thought of seeing Emmaline again terrifies me.'

'You won't have to see her alone. I'll be by your side.'

'The effect would still be the same. All I have to do is think about that woman and my hands go clammy.' This conversation alone had her heart racing in the sick, frightened way it had done all those years ago when she'd walked for hours along the side of the road with her thumb out, praying that whoever stopped for her wouldn't be an axe murderer, no clue where she was going to go or what she was going to do when she got there. She'd been lost and terrified, feelings she remembered all too vividly to ever feel safe from them.

'Emmaline and her evil daughters put me through hell and I will not put myself or our baby through the stress that seeing them again would cause.'

'So you let her win?' he challenged.

Tabitha threw her hands in the air. 'She's already won! I'm not going to put myself through a huge court battle while I'm pregnant.'

His eyes narrowed. 'Once the baby's born? Will you fight her then?'

'Maybe.'

'I don't like the word "maybe". It's weak.'

His comment landed like a wound to her heart. 'Is that what you think of me?'

'No, *matia mou*, it's what you think of yourself. You don't see how strong you are.'

'I'm not strong.'

'The fact you are still here proves you are strong. How many people in your position could have done what you did?'

'I didn't do anything. I've been a chambermaid for years.'

'That takes strength in itself. Think of the girls you were at school with. How many of them would have found the strength to lower their hands into doing the menial work of their household staff? It would be beneath their dignity. Most of them would have ended up on the streets or selling their stories to the tabloid rags for money. You didn't.' He reached across the table to take her hand in his, bringing it up to his face to stare intently at it before turning his gaze back to her. 'You worked your fingers into callouses to support yourself. One day you will find you *do* have the strength to face your stepmother and fight her for what is yours. The power is yours. You just need to believe it.'

Tabitha's heart thumped so hard, there was danger it could burst out of her.

To hear Giannis say those things...

She stared into his eyes and found she could cry to see only sincerity staring back at her.

She'd spent so long thinking herself weak that it was incredible to hear that Giannis, a man who epitomised strength and power, thought her strong.

Her head was still dazed when he brushed a kiss on her knuckles, the gleam returning to his eyes. 'Finish your roll, *koritzi mou*. And then I would suggest you eat another.'

She blinked a couple of times before finding her voice. 'Why would you suggest that?'

'Because I'm taking you back to bed. You will need all your strength for that.' And then he winked and took a huge bite of his apple.

Two weeks after the wedding Giannis was sat in his office reading his investigator's report on Emmaline.

The report on Tabitha had been emailed too but, when he'd hovered over the icon to open it, he'd found himself plagued by a violent bout of nausea and deleted it unread.

His wife deserved better than to have her husband poking into every last detail of her history. It was a violation she had done nothing to warrant and he was sickened with himself for authorising it.

He had no such qualms about reading the report on Emmaline.

By the time he'd finished, reading it a second time for good measure…

He had never felt such fury, not even when he'd received confirmation he was not the father of Anastasia's child.

Emmaline Brigstock was a greater piece of work than even Anastasia had been. The woman was vile. Clever, manipulative and cruel.

Her first husband had died in a motorboat accident when their daughters, Fiona and Saffron, had been small. He'd recognised their names from the guest-list of his ball. Tabitha's tormentors had been there the night they'd conceived their child. Had Tabitha seen them?

He thought of the shattered glass in her hand and knew the answer was yes.

Emmaline's first husband's family described

Emmaline as an arch manipulator. Her own family described her as cold. Her sister, estranged for many years, described her thus: 'the kind of woman children would lovingly follow into her home believing they were going to be shown a litter of puppies, only to watch the puppies be drowned'.

Transcripts of interviews with ex-members of staff who'd borne witness to her treatment of Tabitha—all undertaken on condition of confidentiality—proved that Tabitha's treatment at her stepmother's hand had been far more wretched than she'd confided to Giannis, especially after her father had died. The day after his death, the cook had witnessed Emmaline slap Tabitha around the face. She'd no longer been permitted to eat in the dining room, forced to eat alone in the kitchen. She'd been excluded from all family occasions. Christmas had been spent with the staff. She'd received no presents. Her birthdays had gone unremarked and certainly not celebrated.

Pages and pages of testimony of the cold cruelty Tabitha had endured.

Not a single member of staff had a bad word to say about Tabitha herself. On the contrary, they'd all adored her and had been heartbroken when she'd run away on her eighteenth birthday, all having believed Emmaline's explanation for Tabitha's sudden disappearance from Brigstock Manor.

'She'd been such a happy child but those years after her father died…well…she become a shell of herself,' the housekeeper had explained. 'It was no surprise that she left the moment she legally could. Their treatment of her was barbaric.'

Calling out to his PA to cancel his next meeting, Giannis opened his oak cabinet door and pulled out the bottle of Scotch he kept there for the occasions he worked late and wanted to wind down before returning to his apartment. He filled the glass to the brim, drank half of it then reached for his phone.

First he forwarded the report to his English lawyer with instructions to check for any illegalities in Emmaline's activities. Instinct told him that she must have broken a swathe of English laws.

Then he called his sister.

Niki answered on the first ring.

Cutting out the usual pleasantries, he said, 'It's Tabitha's birthday next week. How do you feel about organising a party for her? I thought we could book that restaurant we took our parents to for their fortieth wedding anniversary.' The restaurant was one of the best in Athens, excellent food, location and atmosphere combined with attentive but relaxed staff, making it a memorable venue for all the right reasons.

Her response was exactly what he had known it would be—enthusiastic—and she promised to get straight on to it.

Knowing he'd put the wheels in motion to bring a smile to his wife's face eased the fury pumping through his blood a little.

What hell she must have lived through.

He imagined a miniature Tabitha, with chubby cheeks and honey-blonde hair, and his heart twisted to think of that little girl losing her mother at such a tender age. Her father had found a new mother for her, and sisters too, not knowing he was bringing a black widow and her venomous offspring into his home.

It would be easy to sneer at her father for falling for Emmaline's lies but Giannis had been the victim of his own gold-digging witch.

Tabitha could not be more different if she tried.

What was she doing right then? Was she reading one of the books he'd had shipped over by an English retailer, after she'd said in passing that she had always loved to read but that she'd only read one book since having been kicked out of her home? It hadn't been time or finances that had stopped her reading. For almost five years she had worked long, physical hours. She'd been too exhausted to read a book. She'd been too exhausted to do anything.

He swiped his phone and found her number before his brain registered what his fingers were doing and he turned it off before he could put the call through.

He downed the rest of his Scotch. The ease he'd just found disappeared. His skin felt suddenly uncomfortable, as if it had tightened around his bones and was constricting his lungs.

Since when did he call a woman just to hear her voice? Never.

And since when did he cut meetings short and cancel appointments just so he could read non-work-related reports? Since when did he focus on anything at work other than the work itself?

Since Tabitha.

It had been the same even before they'd married, he thought, remembering the weeks spent in his fruitless search for her.

In the course of a normal working week he stayed in his apartment in Athens or his other apartments or hotels if he was travelling. He returned to Santorini only at weekends. He worked long hours. Adding an hour's flight at the end of it was a hassle he could do without.

Since their wedding he'd flown back to Santorini six times. He'd had to physically restrain himself from flying back the other times.

He'd meant what he'd said about making their marriage work but there had to be a balance. He'd told himself he had a duty to spend time with his new wife during the week, and not just weekends, but the uncomfortable truth was that he ached to be with her.

She was never far from his mind.

Even with an hour's flight between them the spell she'd woven on him proved strong.

Sooner or later the spell would break.

Tabitha was his wife. He had a duty to provide for her, to protect her and to make life as good and as easy as it could be. He would give her everything she desired. He would treat her like a princess. He would worship her body when he was with her and be faithful when he wasn't.

But his heart he would—must—keep for himself.

Only a fool would allow it to be placed in another's hands after having had it smashed the first time he'd handed it to someone.

CHAPTER TWELVE

THE LATE-SUMMER Santorini heat showed no sign of abating so, while Tabitha's days were spent in glorious sunshine, it was nice to return to the more familiar heat of Vienna.

Tabitha didn't know if she was more excited at seeing her elderly friend or at the fact that she was finally accompanying Giannis somewhere away from Santorini.

In the weeks since their wedding she'd had plenty to keep her occupied but also the luxury of doing nothing if that was what she wanted. After years of toil, proper down time was a true luxury.

It had given her the time she needed to think. About her life, her future and the eternal question of whether Giannis was right that she should fight Emmaline for her inheritance.

He thought she was strong.

She still didn't feel it. She still couldn't picture her stepmother's face without needles of fear pricking on her skin.

Giannis's family all lived close by. If during the working week he stayed away from home for the night she was inundated by them with offers to feed her in their own magnificent homes. Electra, the second-youngest sister and currently on maternity leave, had dropped in a couple of times with her toddler in tow and Niki had taken her out for lunch and kept pressing for another one.

For the first time that she could remember, she wasn't lonely.

But still there lived in her the feeling that something was missing. She just wished she knew what it was.

She missed Giannis when he wasn't there. That could be it. A simple case of missing her husband.

Who wouldn't miss him? He was smart, attentive, sharp-witted, amusing, devilishly handsome and as sexy as sin. She simply couldn't get enough of his love-making. If she had her way they would never leave the bedroom.

But they did have to leave the bedroom, she accepted wistfully.

She just wished she could be with him on the nights he couldn't make it back to Santorini. When she'd suggested she accompany him to Athens, which was his main base during the working week, or wherever else he happened to be business-wise, he'd dismissed it with a, 'You'd be bored'.

She wished, too, that on the nights they spent apart she had any evidence that he missed her. Would it hurt him to pick up the phone and call her? The one time she'd called him, just for a chat, just to hear his voice, he'd been polite but distant.

It felt as if she was deliberately being kept in the shadows of his life. When they were together he couldn't keep his hands off her but when they were apart he didn't spare her a thought.

On the plus side, she had their forthcoming date on Saturday night to look forward to. Giannis was taking her to an exclusive event at the Palvetti production facility in Lake Como. Palvetti was an iconic jewellery and perfumery company, its boss, Alessio, Giannis's oldest and closest friend, the man whose debt Giannis had repaid by throwing the masquerade ball. Tabitha was very much looking forward to going. It would be the first time Giannis had taken her anywhere resembling an actual date since they'd married.

She kept that thought strong inside her when they entered the Basinas Palace Hotel and she found herself wanting to cry when not a single member of staff congratulated them on their marriage.

They didn't know. Unless they looked at the ring on her finger, they would have no reason to think Tabitha was Giannis's wife. Even if they did realise they were married, the hotel staff would look at her and think only that Giannis's new wife looked a lot like one of their old chambermaids.

There had been no announcement of their marriage but she'd thought word must have got out by now that one of Europe's richest men had married, especially after the tragic demise of his first wife. Outside of Giannis's family and his household staff, she doubted anyone knew.

She shoved her darkening thoughts away as she approached Mrs Coulter's door.

Her elderly friend was expecting her.

Tabitha was alarmed at how frail she looked compared to the last time she'd seen her. However, she was in excellent spirits, and after they'd shared a round of sandwiches and a pot of loose-leaf tea she got the playing cards out and insisted on hearing everything that Tabitha had been up to since their last lunch together. She wanted details on everything. How she and Giannis had met, details of the wedding, the whole works.

Tabitha obliged, sparing nothing apart from the bits that could make her blush.

In truth, it felt wonderful to confide it all.

'You're in love!' the elderly woman said, clapping her hands with glee. 'I cannot tell you how happy this makes me.'

'We're not in love,' Tabitha refuted, although her heart had started to thump. 'We married so our baby could have two parents under the same roof.'

'Poppycock. That was an old-fashioned notion even back in my day. That man's rich enough to build you adjoining houses if he'd wanted only for his child to have a mother and father on hand at all times. And you're very naughty for not telling me you spent the night with him at the ball,' she continued. 'You promised me full details, young lady.'

Even though perspiration had broken out on

her back, Tabitha found a smile. 'It was too personal for me to share.'

'First love always is personal, my dear,' Mrs Coulter mused before a dreamy expression drifted over her wizened face. 'I remember my first love. He was a bad boy. My father thought he was scum. He was right—Billy was only interested in one thing—but I didn't care. I thought he was marvellous. The first time we made love was in the shed at the bottom of my garden. My father nearly caught us. He thought foxes had broken in. We only escaped when he went back in the house to get his gun.'

'What happened to him?' Tabitha asked, fascinated at this generations-old tale of young love.

'Who? My father or Billy?'

'Billy.'

Her eyes crinkled with mischief. 'I married him, my dear. Billy was my sweet William. And we had fifty happy years together.'

Could she love Giannis? Was Mrs Coulter right? It was a question still playing in her head four days later when she awoke to find Giannis in bed with her.

'Shouldn't you be at work?' she mumbled with

a sleepy smile. He'd surprised her by flying back from Athens the night before when she'd assumed he'd be staying in his apartment.

He shook his head. There was something smug about the look on his face…

'What?'

His brow creased slightly. 'Don't you know what day it is?'

'Friday?'

'Tabitha, it's your birthday.'

'Oh.'

It had been so long since she'd celebrated that she'd stopped caring about it. It had become nothing but another date on the calendar.

He put his hand under his pillow and pulled out a slim gift-wrapped box. 'Happy birthday, *matia mou.*'

Dumbstruck, Tabitha took it from him with a hand that shook.

She hadn't received a birthday present in seven years.

Giannis, noticing her hesitancy, caught her downcast chin and raised it so he could look at her.

Those beautiful eyes were swimming with tears. 'What's the matter?'

She swallowed and shook her head.

Speaking gently, his guts twisting at what he suspected was the reason for her tears, he said, 'You're not supposed to cry until you've opened it and decided that you hate it—and then you're supposed to cry in private so my ego isn't bruised.'

She managed a smile. 'Is that the law?'

'Nai.'

'I'm sorry for breaking the law.' Then she palmed her hand to his cheek and kissed him. 'Thank you.'

'You haven't opened it yet.'

'Then I will thank you again when I have.'

She took her time opening it, treating the wrapping paper with a respect he'd never seen before. When Giannis had a gift, he ripped into it.

It had been a long time since Tabitha had received a gift of any kind, he suspected.

After taking much longer than the average person would take opening a present, the wrapping was off and she prised the lid open.

Her hand flew to her mouth. When she looked at him again fresh tears were brimming in her eyes. 'Oh, Giannis, it's beautiful. Thank you.'

'It's a bespoke Palvetti creation especially for

you.' He cleared his suddenly tight throat. 'You can wear it tonight.'

'Wear it where?'

'To the restaurant I'm taking you to in Athens.' Taking the box with the gift in it from her hands, he put it on the bedside table and rolled on top of her. He kissed her mouth. 'First, I'm going to make love to you.' He kissed her cheek. 'And then we will eat breakfast.' He kissed her neck. 'And then I will make love to you again. And then we will take my plane to Athens.'

He didn't get any further with his itinerary for the day. Tabitha had hooked her legs tightly around him.

Instead of heading straight to his apartment, Giannis took Tabitha to the Acropolis, where they walked around the great ruins hand in hand, her husband acting as her tour guide as he filled her in on the history of the ancient monument and all the ancient buildings that were a part of it.

Afterwards, they had a late lunch before finally getting to his apartment.

Tabitha had been in it only the once, when they had dropped in after a meeting with his lawyer when they'd been sorting out their pre-nuptial agreement. It was a beautiful, spacious apartment in, naturally, the most affluent area of the city and the contrast to his villa in Santorini was stark.

This time she took no notice of the differences. Her eyes were too busy popping out at the enormous display of roses that covered every available surface.

'I'll have them flown back to Santorini in the morning,' he murmured into her ear as he wrapped his arms around her.

After they'd whiled away the afternoon making love and sharing a bath in his massive sunken tub, they got ready for their meal out.

When she was dressed she asked Giannis to do the clasp on the beautiful choker he'd had made for her.

Gold and covered with gems of all colours in a glimmering pattern, it was the most beautiful item of jewellery she had ever seen.

The next surprise came when they walked into the restaurant and were greeted by his family, all bearing gifts of their own for her.

They were the only guests there. The restaurant had been opened specially for them and decorated with balloons and streamers.

They ate, they drank, music played…there was even a birthday cake for her.

Yet the happiness that had fizzed through her veins that day slowly dissolved as the feeling of being kept in the shadows crept back on her.

Giannis had gone to all this effort for her but had again kept her away from prying eyes. Obviously he wasn't keeping her existence a secret but neither was he flaunting it.

That would change tomorrow, she reminded herself on the drive back to the apartment, when they flew to Lake Como for the Palvetti party.

Everything he'd done for her…

It was incredible.

When they'd ridden the elevator to the top floor, which Giannis owned entirely, and stepped inside his apartment he pulled her into his arms and kissed her. 'I have one more surprise for you,' he murmured.

'A kinky surprise?'

His lips quirked. 'Not quite but I can give you one of those too if you want.'

She admired the tightness of his buttocks as he strode to the bureau and pulled a thick envelope out of a drawer.

'What is it?' she asked when he handed it to her.

'The means for you to fight back. Evidence of your stepmother's fraudulent behaviour.'

Stunned, she clutched the envelope to her chest. 'How did you get this?'

'I had Emmaline investigated.' A muscular arm slid around her waist and pulled her to him. His breath was warm against her hair. 'When you are ready to fight and reclaim what is yours, I will be there to help you. You don't have to do this alone.'

'So you don't think I'm strong.'

'Being strong does not mean having to do things alone. This is the ammunition you need for when you are ready to confront her. You have much strength, *matia mou*. You just have to believe it.'

Tabitha pressed her cheek to his chest and listened to the steady beat of his heart echo in her ears and vibrate through her skin.

At that moment her own heart had bloomed enough to burst.

Tabitha did not think she had ever been so happy in her entire life. Possibly when she'd been a small child before her mother had died, but as she could hardly remember that far back she couldn't really count it.

Certainly not since, though.

That morning they flew from Athens to Milan but, instead of touring the city, they spent the day in bed in Giannis's magnificent Milanese apartment, only surfacing when it was time to get ready for the Palvetti party.

The envelope he'd given her sat in her over-sized handbag. She had yet to open it but every time she caught a glimpse or brushed it with her fingers her heart filled with such love for him it choked her.

Because, of course, Mrs Coulter was right. Tabitha loved her husband. She'd loved him from the moment he'd taken her into his arms and waltzed her around that wonderful dance floor and she wasn't going to deny it to herself a moment longer.

Lying in the foamy water of his huge roll-topped bath, her back pressed against his sopping chest, his fingers making lazy circles around her nipples, the need to declare her feelings was strong.

She'd never told anyone who wasn't her parent that she loved them.

How would he react when she did declare herself? Surely, *surely*, Mrs Coulter was right and he had strong feelings for her too? All the effort he'd gone to for her birthday, his anger at Emmaline's treatment of her, the fact he'd hired an investigator to prove her stepmother's fraud, his inability to keep his hands off her...surely that all meant something?

His hand moved lower to stroke her softly swelling belly. She turned her head to place a kiss on his biceps.

And then she twisted round to kiss his mouth.

Tonight, she thought as she sank onto his length and gasped at the incredible feelings flooding through her, feelings she just could not get enough of.

She would tell him her feelings tonight.

Giannis sucked in a breath when Tabitha finally emerged from their bedroom. After their steamy bath, he'd shaved and donned his suit, then worked his way through his email inbox while she'd got herself ready.

Tonight, wearing a sparkly deep blue dress that accentuated her growing curves in all the right places, the choker he'd had custom-made for her birthday snug around her neck, that glow that must be innate in her shone brighter than ever.

She never failed to take his breath away.

'You look beautiful, *glikia mou.*'

Colour stained her rounded cheeks and she bestowed him with a smile of such brilliance it dazzled him.

Something sharp pierced through his chest and then, without any warning, his heart began to thud. But these erratic beats were different, heavier than the thundering beats he'd become accustomed to with Tabitha.

These beats vibrated to the tips of his toes and filled him with such an ache that alarm bells clanged loudly in his head and he stopped midstep towards her.

After an age passed he loosened his shoulders and pulled out his phone to instruct his driver to collect them.

Despite the motion sickness Tabitha's first helicopter ride induced, she found herself enchanted by her first glimpse of the Palvetti production facility. Nestled between two mountains in Lake Como, it appeared through the darkness of the night sky in shimmering white lights looking more like a castle than anything else, including the monastery it had started its life as.

The moment they touched down, a limousine appeared.

They were driven past masses of security to a huge courtyard and then they passed through scanners and she found herself in the midst of a select number of people whose faces she recognised as some of the wealthiest in the world. They were all clearly buzzing to be there: the first ever visitors at the facility behind one of the world's most iconic brands.

A touch intimidated, she reached for the security of Giannis's hand. He gave it a quick squeeze then dropped it to stride forward and embrace his old friend Alessio Palvetti. Disappointment lashed her when he introduced them and made not so much as a passing reference to her being his wife.

She told herself it was because there was no time, and that he would introduce her properly later, for Alessio called for everyone's attention and announced the start of the tour.

Moments later, she found herself dumbstruck. It felt as though she'd stepped into a futuristic sci-fi film. She had never seen so much white:

floors, ceilings, walls, not a mark to be seen. Contained within the whiteness were laboratories, indoor greenhouses, testing rooms…

As they toured the vast, deliciously scented rooms, their guide, a Palvetti whose name she'd already forgotten, touched on the history of the company in almost mythical terms. Tabitha's only disappointment was that they weren't invited into the workshop part of the facility where their wonderful jewellery was created. She lightly fingered the beautiful choker that Giannis had bought her for her birthday, which glittered with diamonds, emeralds and rubies, awed that it was the incredibly talented brains within this compound who'd made it for her.

When the tour was over, they were led into a vast yet surprisingly intimate room so different from the corridors and laboratories they had just walked that for a moment it felt as if she'd stepped back in time to Italy's mediaeval past.

Thick velvet gold drapes hung on the exposed ancient stone walls, crystal chandeliers hung on the frescoed ceiling and gold life-sized statues stood in each corner while a string quartet played jaunty yet sophisticated background music. Stunning models dressed in silver and adorned with

Palvetti jewellery carried trays of canapés, champagne and, mercifully, alcohol-free drinks.

Ravenous though she was, Tabitha found herself feeling too tight inside to eat.

Giannis had kept by her side throughout the tour but the easy affection he displayed when alone with her was nowhere to be found. She had the distinct impression he was avoiding her touch. He was certainly avoiding touching her.

There were only twenty guests and a handful of Palvettis yet somehow he managed not to mention their marital state to any of them. She caught a few curious eyes clock her left hand but these people were the cream of high society and it would have been the height of poor manners to ask a stranger, which she was to them, if the gold band she wore on her wedding finger was a wedding ring.

Her mood lowered further when Giannis discussed business with an Agon prince in his native language. She could hardly use her phone app to translate for her benefit in this situation, so she was forced to stand decoratively beside them pretending that she didn't feel like a wallflower.

Mercifully, Alessio's new wife Beth, a fellow

English girl, took pity on her. Though her eyes were alight with curiosity, they had a lovely long chat about Tabitha's new necklace, which Beth recognised as a Palvetti, and about Beth's new role within the company. Discovering that Beth was the brains behind this event, Tabitha found herself envious that her fellow countryman had settled into this world so well and so quickly. Or had she? She noticed that Beth's eyes kept flickering to her husband, the tiniest crease on her face, as if she were concerned about something.

By the time the evening came to a close, Tabitha's mood was as low as it had been the morning of their wedding. Not even the goody bag she'd been handed—which contained a beautiful gold and emerald bracelet and a perfume set with her name on the packaging, with a note in beautiful calligraphy stating all the contents had been made especially for her—could lift it.

They'd spent their first evening together in the company of Giannis's peers, some of whom he considered good friends, and he had not made a single allusion to their marriage.

CHAPTER THIRTEEN

'WHAT'S THE MATTER?' Giannis asked when they were back inside his Milanese apartment. Tabitha had hardly said two words to him since they'd left Lake Como. When he'd asked if she'd enjoyed herself, she'd raised one slim shoulder in a half-hearted shrug.

Troubled cornflower eyes connected with his before she turned her back to him, kicked her shoes off and headed to the kitchen.

'Tabitha?'

She opened a cupboard and removed a cup. 'What?'

'Something is bothering you. Talk to me.'

Instead of answering, she filled the cup with water, drank it, refilled it and drank again. Only when she'd put the empty cup on the draining board did she face him.

Folding her arms across her waist, she stared at him silently.

Now he was the one to ask, 'What?'

Her eyes narrowed before she bluntly asked, 'Are you ashamed of me?'

Taken aback at the ludicrous question, he laughed and pulled her into his arms. 'Of course not.'

She made no attempt to return his embrace, her frame as stiff as a mannequin's.

'You didn't touch me all night,' she said, her voice as stiff as her frame.

Tabitha was pregnant, he reminded himself. When his sister Helena had been pregnant, her hormones had made her irrational enough times that Giannis had felt sorry for her husband. He'd been lucky that, up to this point, Tabitha had been nothing but rational and considered. Outside of the bedroom, that was. In the bedroom, she was a vixen, as much a slave to their desire as he was.

'It was business,' he explained with a murmur, nuzzling into her delectable neck, fingers sliding up her back to find the zip. He was already rock-hard for her.

Theos, when *wasn't* he hard for her? Sharing the same air as her but not being able to touch her had been a masochistic form of torture but a necessary one after the violent emotions that had pulsed through him before they'd left the apartment. To master his control he needed space from her. Being surrounded by company that evening had given him the distance he'd needed to regain control of himself and, now they were alone again, he could hardly wait to…

She put a hand to his shoulder and pushed him back an inch. 'No it wasn't.'

'Most of the guests there were business associates of mine. It was not the place for displays of affection.' This wasn't a lie, he assured himself. Not the whole truth but certainly not a lie.

'So you feel affection for me, do you?'

Groping her bottom, he pressed her to him so she could feel his excitement. 'There, *matia mou*,' he whispered into her ear, her scent dancing straight into his bloodstream. 'Solid evidence of my affection for you.'

'Sex, you mean. You can have that with anyone.' Then she ducked out from his hold and walked out of the kitchen.

Perplexed, loins throbbing, he followed her into the living room. 'Do you want me to order food?' he asked carefully. 'You didn't eat much this evening. You must be hungry.' Which was probably what was making her irritable.

She sat on the sill of the bay window and crossed her legs. 'You noticed?'

Propping himself against the wall, he flashed the smile that normally made her grin. 'You must know by now that I notice everything.'

Her stony expression didn't alter. 'I notice things too. Like that you didn't once refer to me as your wife tonight.'

'Tonight wasn't about us.'

'That shouldn't stop you telling people—your friends—that you've married and that you're going to be a father.'

'I didn't think you would want people outside of the family to know about the baby until the first trimester was clear.'

'You could have discussed that with me first but, regardless, it shouldn't stop you telling people that you've married again. We've been married for three weeks. Tonight is the first time I've met any of your friends. Alessio is your best friend and you seemed pretty pally with that prince you were talking to too. Did you tell either of them we're married?'

'As I just said, tonight wasn't about us.' He found himself speaking through gritted teeth.

'Tonight was a big deal for Alessio and it wouldn't have been right to take the attention away from him.'

Again, this might not be the whole truth but it certainly wasn't a lie. Announcing that he and Tabitha had married would have caused a stir amongst his peers but he'd planned to mention it casually. Before the words could form, however, he'd remembered the fanfare of his marriage to Anastasia which they had all been privy to and a cold chill had run down his spine at how it had all ended.

'So when are you planning to tell people?'

'People know. I've not hidden that we're married to anyone—all anyone has to do is look at my wedding ring to see that I'm married.'

'Your family know but if you weren't so close I doubt you'd even have invited them to our wedding. You didn't want to include anyone else.'

'You didn't want to invite anyone apart from Mrs Coulter,' he reminded her.

His visions of returning to the apartment and ripping Tabitha's clothes off, fantasies that had burned through him the entire night, had been doused in ice. Tabitha had ambushed him with a conversation he'd been completely unprepared for and it was clear it was heading in a direction in which he did not want to go.

'That's because I have no one left who really matters to me. You do. You have a whole network of friends and far more family than even those you invited. How many of them know about my existence?'

'The ones who matter—my immediate family—but I have no objection to people knowing we're married.' He strode to the bar in the corner of the room. 'Eventually anyone who needs to know will know because we took our vows for life.'

He grabbed a bottle of Scotch. The first drops of liquid hit the glass when Tabitha, quietly but with a large dose of steel in her husky voice, said, 'What do you feel for me?'

Perspiration broke out on his back. 'You know what I feel for you. Don't I show it in every possible way?'

'You're talking about sex again.'

'Sex is important.'

'Only if it comes with emotions. When we're not together, when you're alone in your Athens apartment…do you even think about me?'

He tipped the Scotch down his throat and fought to hear his own voice above the suddenly ferocious beats of his heart. 'Of course I do.'

'Then why do you never call?'

The echoes from his heart now drummed in his head. 'I didn't know you wanted me to.'

'I want you to *want* to call me.' Tabitha's exasperation was fleeting, her stomach too knotted for anything to hold inside her. This was a conversation she wished desperately that she hadn't started but one she knew it was essential to have. 'How can we sustain a life together if all there is between us is good sex?'

'It's a damn sight more than a lot of other couples have, but that's not all we have. We'll have a child too.'

'What about love?' she challenged, an icy chill creeping down her spine. 'Where does that come into it?'

He froze right before her eyes but not before a look of abject horror flashed across his face, freezing his features with the rest of him.

It was a look that spoke a thousand words.

Then the horror vanished as quickly as it had appeared and he nonchalantly poured himself another drink. 'I told you from the start that I don't want love. I've been there...'

'I know. It tastes bitter,' she finished for him. The room began to spin and she had to grind her toes into the carpet to keep herself upright. Hoarsely, she added, 'Yes, I remember you saying that, but so much has happened between us since you said it that I foolishly hoped your feelings towards me had changed.'

'Of course they've changed. Things have been great between us but I've never made false promises to you. I've never lied to you. We married for our child.'

Her entire body now cold but her brain *burning*, she stared at him for the longest time as everything became clear to her.

She'd fallen in love with this man the night they'd conceived their child. Her feelings for him since had been like a runaway train on an incline and she found herself hurtling towards a sheer drop at the end of the track. If she didn't pull the brake now she would plunge over the edge headfirst onto the jagged rocks below.

He gazed back at her, gripping his glass, knuckles white.

She swallowed the sharp lump lodged in her

throat. 'My feelings for you are simple,' she said slowly. 'I want your heart and I want you to be as proud and happy to call me your wife as I am to call you my husband. I want everything, Giannis, but I can see that it's not possible for me to have it. I think for both our sakes, and our child's sake, we should call it quits.'

'What the hell are you talking about?' He was staring at her as if she'd suddenly sprouted a second head.

'That I think we should cut our losses and end things now while we can keep things amicable.'

Anger darkened his features and he slammed his glass on the bar. 'No! You do not get to call it quits because I don't call you. If you're not happy with something, you talk about it and we deal with it.'

'I *am* talking to you but your answers are only confirming my worst fears. We are never going to have the marriage I want.'

Like a panther stalking its prey, he prowled towards her. 'I've given you everything you've asked of me. I've arranged for our child to have everything on my death, I only have eyes for you and intend to remain faithful for the rest of our lives—what more can you possibly want?'

Somehow she managed to get her watery legs to stand and face him. 'I want to feel that, even if there was no baby in my belly, you and I would still be here.'

'We're only here *because* of the baby. That is a fact, *matia mou.*' Before she knew what was happening, he had her pressed against the wall. His breath was hot against her ear, hot enough to seep through her skin and melt her love-sick bones. 'The night we created our child was the best of my life, surpassed only by the other nights we've shared since we married. I want you more than I have ever wanted anyone. The nights I'm apart from you I fantasise about making love to you. My blood burns for you...and I know your blood burns for me.' And then, as if proving his point, he crushed her mouth and kissed her, filling her senses with his dark taste.

For a few glorious moments she sank into the heat of his mouth, a small fix like a shot of caffeine to temper all the torrid emotions swirling inside her.

Heat pulsed through her, hard, strong, undeniable. Her aching body taking control, she hooked her arms around his neck, her lips parted...

And then sanity crashed through her harder than the caffeine shot and she wrenched her mouth away and pushed her hands to his chest. *'No!'*

With a muttered curse he stepped back, brow creased in confusion, breathing heavily.

'I know you want me *here*,' she cried, placing her hand on his groin, feeling for the very last time the strength of his desire for her before moving her hand and placing it on his chest. The thuds of his heart were heavy beneath her palm and she could have screamed with the anguish of what she must do.

'But I want you to want me *here* too, in your heart. I want you to call me when we're not together because you need to hear my voice. I want you to miss me when we're not together as much as I miss you. I want you to take me with you when you travel because you can't bear to be parted from me but, the truth is, if I'm not with you then I don't exist for you. Your feelings for me are all wrapped up in your desire for me and when that fades what are we going to be left with?'

He dragged his fingers violently through his

hair, a tumult of emotions flickering over his face. 'No one knows what the future holds.'

'And you're not denying anything I've just said! We could have something really special here but you're not even prepared to try.' And, as she said the words, fury laced her veins and she shoved hard at his chest with all the pain ravaging her heart. 'You won't try because you're a coward. Love turned bitter for you with Anastasia so you're punishing me for it by refusing to embrace what we have.'

'That is the most ridiculous thing I have ever heard you say,' he snarled. 'I'm not punishing you for anything. You've been insecure about Anastasia from the start. How many times do I have to tell you—whatever feelings I had for that woman died the day I learned another man had fathered her child!'

'But at least you *had* feelings for her before it all turned to hate. You've punished me for her sins since the day I told you I was pregnant! It's infected every part of our relationship because you refuse to let go of your hate for her and embrace a future with me.'

His face whitened, the pulse on his jaw throbbing madly.

'I want happiness, Giannis, and I can't have that if I'm spending my life waiting for your interest in me to fade while holding on to the futile hope that one day you'll let me into your heart. I've spent enough of my life living in the shadows and having my very existence denied and I'm not prepared to go through it any more. I can't hold on to a dream that doesn't exist. If you can't even try to let go of the past and embrace a true future with me then I leave now.'

He grabbed hold of her arm and pulled her back to him. 'I'm not letting you go. You're my *wife*.'

'Then start treating me like your wife.' She yanked her arm from his hold. 'You think I want to go? This is breaking my heart, Giannis, but if I stay as things stand it's going to destroy me.'

The darkness shadowed his face again, his features contorting with a mixture of menace and anguish. 'I'm not letting you take my child from me.'

'I'm not taking it from you.' She kneaded her temples and blinked back the hot tears, terrified to unleash them. 'You're still its father, but right now it's being nurtured in my belly, and until it's born I will care for it.'

'What about the stable life we married to provide it with? If you leave then everything we've done will have been for nothing.'

'No, Giannis, it won't have been for nothing.' Hating to see the pain on his face, even though she knew his pain wasn't for her but their child, she flung her arms around his neck for the last time and pressed the lightest of kisses to his mouth. Then she stared into the clear blue eyes brimming with all the emotion she wished could be for her. 'It's for our baby's sake as much as mine that I must do this. I don't want it to live with a mother who's miserable all the time. Better he or she has two happy parents even if they are apart. You're the one who's taught me to be strong and the strength you've given me will make me a far better mother than I would have been.'

The strength he'd given her had also given her the spine she needed to put her future in her own hands.

She pulled away from him, no longer able to look at him, and walked out of the living room.

He followed her to the front door as she was hooking her handbag over her shoulder. Luckily her passport was already in it.

'Where will you go?' he asked stiffly.

'Back to England.' She blinked back the tears still fighting for release and swallowed. 'I'm going to do what you keep telling me to do and fight for what is mine. I'm going to get my inheritance back for me and our baby.'

He shut the door before she'd made it to the elevator.

She could do this. She was strong as Giannis had told her.

Leaving him had proved it as nothing else could.

She would not be second best any more. And she would not allow her inheritance and her child's inheritance to be stolen from her a minute longer.

She wouldn't even bang on the door.

This was her home. She had no intention of waiting politely for entry to be granted.

She took one deep breath and turned the handle.

The moment she crossed the threshold, Tabitha's bravado almost deserted her. Her palms went clammy and her heart began that awful sick thud of dread.

She closed her eyes and took another deep breath. Clearing her throat, she parted her lips, but before she could call out her stepmother appeared.

For a moment neither of them said anything, then the frigid mask that was Emmaline's Botoxed face spoke. 'What are you doing here?'

Tabitha wiped her hands on her trousers and fought for air.

'What are you doing here?' Emmaline repeated icily.

In desperation Tabitha brought Giannis's face to mind and his stern assurance that she was strong enough to confront her stepmother and reclaim what was hers.

This was something she *had* to do.

Ignoring the tremors in her hand, she pulled out the document from her bag and held it out.

'What is that?' Emmaline sneered.

Tabitha cleared her throat and looked her square in the eye. 'Copies of the documentary proof I've obtained that you used fraudulent methods to evict me from my home and steal my inheritance.'

Giannis's investigative team had been more thorough than she could have imagined.

She'd read through it in the hotel suite she'd checked into in England six days ago, the day after she'd left him. She was still using the hotel as her base and had no intention of leaving until her home was her own again and she could move back to the place she belonged.

She had to keep ignoring the voice that kept whispering Santorini was where she belonged.

Emmaline's mouth dropped open. Now she was the one struggling to speak.

Tabitha straightened and lifted her chin. 'I'm here to give you notice. You have one week to leave this house and transfer all my father's assets into my name or I call the police and have you prosecuted for theft and fraud.'

'You can't do that.'

'Every time you argue with me, I decrease it by a day. This house is not yours. It was never yours. You had no right to it and you always knew that—this house belonged to my mother. My father transferred it into her name when I was a baby as a gift to her and she bequeathed it to me when she became ill.'

Her parents *had* protected her inheritance. When it had been clear her mother couldn't survive, they'd drawn up a separate trust for the house which allowed her father to live in it for the rest of his life, but the ownership of it would become Tabitha's. He'd intended to surprise her with this when she turned twenty-one.

She knew why Emmaline had thought she could get away with stealing it. She'd thought Tabitha weak and she'd been right.

Not any more. Tabitha would never allow anyone to walk over her again. She would never again accept that things were the way they were and that all you could do was endure and survive.

She wanted to live.

'You stole my home from me and I have documentary proof that you stole much more too. All you're entitled to is half of the income from the brewery. Considering you have had all that income for your greedy self these past five years, you can have no objection to signing the document that's also enclosed transferring your share into my name.'

She didn't have to threaten her again. The rouge on Emmaline's cheeks was stark against the whiteness of her cheeks.

'One week,' Tabitha said sweetly as she turned back to the door to leave. 'You know what you have to do. Oh, and before I go, send my love to your daughters.'

Walking back down the long gravelled driveway, fallen autumn leaves crunching beneath her feet, she climbed into the waiting taxi without looking back.

Only when the driver pulled onto the narrow backroad did her posture dissolve and the adrenaline that had carried her through the ordeal slump.

Before all her courage deserted her, she snatched her phone out of her bag and, after deliberating how best to phrase it, fired off a message to Giannis.

I've seen Emmaline. She'll be gone from the house in a week. Thank you for your help.

However things had ended between them, he'd done this for her. He'd gathered the evidence she needed to reclaim her inheritance and helped her find the strength she needed to confront Emmaline.

She would call him soon and speak to him but she wasn't ready for that yet. Her strength could only take her so far and, until she knew she could be in a room with him without falling to her knees and begging him to take her back, it was best she kept her distance.

But, God, she missed him. All that had kept her going this past week had been gearing herself up for that confrontation with her stepmother. It had given her a focus that had dulled the ache she carried in every cell of her body.

She would not go back to him. She couldn't. She could not live her life by his side knowing her love would never be reciprocated. Eventually it would destroy her. And what kind of example would it set for her child? She wanted her child to find love and fulfilment. One day she hoped to find it for herself too.

CHAPTER FOURTEEN

'WHAT ARE YOU doing here?'

Niki barged her way past Giannis uninvited. 'I'm going on a date and thought I'd see if Tabitha was in—I want to borrow that gorgeous choker you got her for her birthday. Is she here?'

'She's gone,' he answered baldly, his stomach clenching.

'Gone where?'

He shrugged again. It was easier than talking. In the week since Tabitha had walked out on him in Milan, he'd found his vocal cords too tight to make more than monotonous grunts. After a merciful week doing business in Toronto away from his inquisitive family, five hours back in Santorini and his peace was shattered.

'When will she be back?'

Another shrug.

'Have you turned into a mute?' Not waiting for an answer, she strolled through to his bar and began rummaging through the rows of liqueurs, spirits and wines. 'You're running low on white wine,' she observed cheerfully as she pulled a bottle of white out of the fridge. 'How did the party go?'

'What party?' he asked tiredly.

'Alessio's party.'

'It wasn't a party. It was a function.' And it felt like a lifetime ago.

She poked her tongue at him and poured them both a large glass. 'How did the "function" go?'

'Fine.'

'What did Alessio say when you told him you'd got married again? Was he cross that he wasn't invited?'

He took the glass she thrust in his hand and took a large drink of it. 'The subject didn't come up.'

'Why not? And if you give another shrug as an answer I'm going to punch you.' But before he could answer Niki's eyes narrowed as she looked properly at him. 'When was the last time you had a shave?'

'What?'

She put her face to his neck then pulled away with her nose wrinkling. 'You need a shower too.' Then she stilled and bit her lip. 'Giannis… where's Tabitha?'

The clenching in his stomach became a vice as he finally admitted, 'I don't know.'

'What do you mean, you don't know?'

His heart twisted so tightly he had to force the words out. 'She's left me.'

And she hadn't come back. All her clothes, her jewellery, her cosmetics, every single item he'd bought her, were still in her dressing room. She had money he'd given her in her bank account and, from the message he'd received a few hours ago—the first message she'd sent since leaving—had her house back.

She had no reason to come home to him.

The horror on his sister's face landed like a punch in his guts and he struggled to drag air into his lungs.

'What happened?' she eventually whispered.

'A difference of opinion.'

He could feel Niki's troubled eyes on him as he paced the vast living area—a space that had grown disproportionately since Tabitha had gone, enhancing her absence—to stand outside on the terrace overlooking the sea.

Far in the distance he spotted a yacht. He kept his gaze fixed on it when his sister joined him.

Something hot and rancid had been building up in him, right from the pit of his stomach, for days. He'd smothered it and doused it but now he could feel it rising sharply inside him.

Niki sighed and placed her hand on his.

But her attempt at comfort felt like needles on his skin and he snatched his hand away.

'Is it fixable?' she asked quietly.

He shrugged.

She punched him on the arm.

'What was that for?' he growled.

'I did warn you I would punch you if you shrugged another answer. Tell me what happened.'

'I don't want to talk about it.' He downed the rest of his wine.

There was a long period of silence before she said, 'What are you going to do to get her back?'

'Nothing. She doesn't want to be with me any more.'

'Don't be stupid. She's crazy about you.'

His breath grew ragged and he gritted his teeth. 'We married to legitimise our child. It is disappointing that things haven't worked out but we are both agreed that we will continue to put our child's best interests first.'

'And you're happy with this? Because from where I'm standing you look as miserable as sin. Did you sleep in those clothes?'

The build-up of rage in his stomach suddenly exploded. Turning on his favourite sister, Giannis shouted, 'For once in your life can you keep your nose out of my affairs? My marriage is none of your business. Tabitha is none of your business. *I'm* none of your business, so do us both a favour and get out of my face and go meet your date.'

Niki was nothing if not his sister, and uttered words at him that would have once earned her a slap from their mother. 'What is wrong with you, Giannis? Where's the fearless brother I've always adored? You love Tabitha…'

'Love has *nothing* to do with our marriage.'

'Oh, get over yourself, you blind fool. Anyone can see you're crazy about each other, but instead of getting out there and doing everything in your power to bring her home you're moping like a love-sick teenager. Tabitha is the best thing that ever happened to you and if you're too stupid to see that and apologise for whatever you've done to make her leave then you really don't deserve her.'

'You automatically put the blame on me?' he roared.

'She left *you* which, yes, does imply that you're to blame. Tabitha loves you. There is no way she would have left if she didn't think she had no alternative...'

He couldn't listen to another word. With a roar that seemed to come from the depths of his soul, Giannis hurled the glass over the wall and onto the jagged rocks below where it shattered into a thousand shards.

It was the perfect mimicry of his own shattered heart.

A week later and Brigstock Manor was Tabitha's again.

Emmaline and her daughters were gone, as was most of the garish furniture they'd replaced her parents' furniture with.

Tabitha kept wandering through the mostly empty rooms as if she were in a dream. It didn't feel real.

This was her home. This was the place where all the ghosts of her past lived. The echo of her mother's laugh, the one thing she remembered about her with any clarity, was contained in these walls. Everything else about her parents had been erased. A part of her wanted to confront Emmaline and demand she replace everything she'd thrown away but her thickening waistline was all she needed to dissuade herself.

She had her home back. She would receive a regular income from the business and, after her child was born, she would do that business degree she'd always wanted to do and eventually take her rightful place on the Brigstock Brewery board.

Everything was going in the right direction. Now it was time to live her life again.

She just wished she didn't feel so lonely.

She wished she didn't still miss Giannis so much.

She still hadn't found the courage to call him. They'd exchanged a few polite messages about her health and the baby but nothing more than that.

She feared hearing his voice. But she heard it in her dreams, every single night. She would reach out for him in her sleep, the tears spilling before she could stop them.

She never cried when she was awake.

Three days after taking possession of the manor and hiring a cleaning firm to come in and blitz the place—she might be a master cleaner but this was a job much too big for her—she decided to get out of the cleaning crew's way and take a look in the attic. Maybe Emmaline had forgotten about the Brigstock stuff that had been stored up there for generations and had left it unharmed.

Checking her watch first—a specialist decorating firm was coming over later to give her a quote on redecorating the manor back to its original glory—she climbed the creaky narrow stairs that led to it and opened the hatch.

The attic covered the entire ceiling space. Tabitha remembered poking her head in it as a child and being frightened of the shadows.

What a scared little girl she had been to be frightened of shadows. No wonder her stepsisters had found her such an easy target to terrorise.

Judging from the dust that swirled in the air as she walked through it, no one had been in the attic in years, but she was cheered to find old furniture in there: a chesterfield sofa and armchair, a dressing table and wardrobe that would have been fashionable in the nineteenth century, a variety of ottomans amongst other smaller items and dozens and dozens of boxes.

A short while later, she opened the lid of another ottoman and found a nest of white lace. Her mother's wedding dress and Tabitha's christening outfit.

Hands shaking, she hugged the wedding dress to her chest and carried it to the full-length mirror carelessly left against one of the walls.

This was the dress her mother had worn the day she'd married her father, the day her father had once whispered had been the second-happiest of his life. The happiest had followed three years later when Tabitha had been born.

Suddenly she found her legs could hold her up no more and she sank onto the floor, tears flowing down her cheeks as if a dam had burst.

She would trade everything to have them back for just one day. One hour. One minute.

If they'd been there she would have had their comforting arms around her easing the pain of her broken heart.

Oh, she *missed* him. That so-called great healer called Time hadn't healed anything. She missed Giannis's smile, his laughter, his sardonic wit, his love-making, his tenderness. Everything. She missed everything. Her arms ached to hold him and touch him. She longed to see him—had to resist searching his name on her phone just as she had to resist speaking to him. She had never known pain like it and it tore at her then, in a way she'd fought letting it tear at her before, shredding her already broken heart.

Only when there was a loud bang on the attic hatch did she drag herself off the floor.

'Miss Brigstock?' came the voice of one of the cleaners. 'You have a visitor.'

'Tell him I'll be down in a minute,' she called back, hurriedly wiping her face. It must be the decorator.

She winced to see her reflection. Her face was puffy, her eyes red from crying.

So much for crying being cathartic. The first time she'd cried in over a fortnight and she felt worse than ever.

Neatly folding the dress back into the ottoman, she re-tied her loose ponytail, wiped the dust from her clothes and headed back down the narrow stairs.

Moving through to the drawing room where he would be waiting for her, she almost had a heart attack when she walked in and found Giannis sitting there stiffly on the window ledge.

Struck mute, she could only stare at him, heart thumping into immediate overdrive.

Their eyes connected and in that moment a wave of emotion so strong pulsed through her that she pressed her back to the wall to keep herself upright.

'Hello, Tabitha.'

Just to hear her name fall from his lips was enough to make her veins dance and she crossed her arms tightly across her chest, grinding her feet to the floor, doing everything in her power to stop her treacherous body from flying over to fling herself at him.

She cleared her tight throat and forced herself to speak. 'This is an unexpected surprise.'

But not a welcome one, Giannis suspected ruefully.

He stared at the beautiful face that had haunted his every waking moment for what felt like for ever and felt his heart rip.

She looked like she'd been crying.

'What brings you here?' She spoke politely but he heard the rawness in her voice.

'I wanted to see you…see the home you grew up in. Is something the matter, *matia mou*?'

Her shoulders rose and, though she pulled a rueful face, she blinked numerous times, as if trying to hold back more tears. 'I just found my mother's wedding dress in the attic.'

She'd been in the attic? That explained the dust clinging to the slender frame that had thickened a touch in the seventeen days since he'd last seen her.

Chin wobbling, she pulled at her ponytail. 'Can I get you a drink? I don't have any alcohol but I've got tea and coffee.'

'No, thank you.'

'A tour of the house?' She didn't wait for a response, springing away from the door and heading straight out of the room.

Without ceremony she guided him quickly through the many rooms of the sprawling manor house. He didn't need to close his eyes to imagine Tabitha as a small child running happily through the spacious rooms, her happiness coming to a crashing end when her father had married the stepmother from hell.

He didn't make any comment until she opened a door on the first floor and muttered, 'This was

Fiona's room.' Then she muttered something under her breath and stepped inside it to snatch something from under the bed.

She held the photograph up with a frown. 'I can add this to the bonfire.'

He looked at the three faces staring into the camera's lens and shuddered. All three were pretty—beautiful, even—and immaculately made up but their eyes were empty.

'Your stepfamily make the witches of Macbeth look like angels,' he quipped, trying to break the tension radiating from her. He hadn't come here to distress her.

She gave a bark of laughter and wiped a stray tear from her cheek as she walked out of the room. 'The witches of Macbeth would have been easier to live with,' she said over her shoulder but before she could walk away he put his hand on her shoulder.

It was an instinctive action that came from a hand that had yearned to touch her from the moment she had stepped into the drawing room.

'I'm proud of you,' he said in a low voice, dropping his hand to hang uselessly by his side. 'You defeated the witches. I hope you can be happy now.'

Her rigid torso didn't move. 'I couldn't have done it without your help.'

'You would have. Everything my investigators discovered, you would have found out for yourself in your own time.'

He could hear her breathing.

Long moments passed before she rolled her shoulders and turned to face him.

'You should go,' she said quietly. 'I've got decorators coming over to give me a quote and a hundred other things I need to be getting on with.'

She gave him no time to answer, walking away from him to the end of the corridor and disappearing from his view down the ancient cantilevered stairs.

Throat closed, he followed her until he stood at the top of the stairs and she was taking the final step at the bottom.

'I fell in love with you when I saw you walking the stairs of my palace hotel,' he called to her.

Her foot hovered mid-air, hand tightening on the banister.

'You enchanted me from that first glance. When I found you gone the next morning... I spent weeks trying to find you.'

Slowly she turned to look up at him, her expression disbelieving.

Putting one foot before the other, Giannis reached into his pocket and pulled out the one reminder she'd left of their night together until she'd walked back into his life.

When he reached her at the bottom of the stairs he held it out to her in his open hand without speaking.

Slowly she plucked the earring from him and stared at it.

Then shining cornflower eyes stared at him.

'I have carried that with me every day since that night,' he told her. 'I could not forget you. I tried. God knows I tried, but you were with me all the time, in my head, in my heart... I could not forget you. It's been the same since you left me but so much worse. You're in my head, *matia mou*, under my skin and in my heart. I have missed you more than I thought it was possible to miss another.'

To Tabitha's utter bewilderment, he sank down onto his knees before her and took her hand in his.

'Since you left me I can't breathe properly and

I am here to ask you—to beg you—to please give me another chance.'

His words were like nectar to a starving, exhausted bee but Tabitha had been through too much, had wrung her heart out too much over him, to believe that the dream she had for them could come true.

She pulled her hand from his hold and stepped back. 'I'm sorry, Giannis, I want to believe you...'

He closed his eyes. His throat moved a number of times. 'You were right that I kept you at a distance. When I'm with you my feelings overwhelm me. I needed to keep control. I never lost control of my feelings with Anastasia but her infidelity still shattered me. What I felt for her... I won't insult you by downplaying it but my feelings for her were nothing compared with what I feel for you. I'm not going to lie—they terrified me. I never called you when we were apart, not because I didn't want to, but because I was trying to prove to myself that I didn't need you. The truth is, every minute spent apart from you was spent missing you and needing you.'

Tabitha covered her mouth. She wanted to

cover her ears too but the nectar coming from his mouth was too sweet to resist.

Her aching, broken heart yearned to believe him.

He rose back to his feet and closed the space she had created between them.

'I spent our marriage trying to free myself from the spell you'd put me under, but I was a fool, because I couldn't see that it wasn't a spell of your creation but a spell binding us both.' Giannis took both her rigid hands in his and pulled them to his chest so she could feel the aching thuds of his heart. 'You felt it too, didn't you?'

The shining eyes finally spilled into tears and she gave an almost imperceptible nod that gave him the strength to continue.

'This heart beats only for you. You have my heart, my body and my soul. Without you I am nothing. I love you, *matia mou*, and if it takes me the rest of my life to make you believe that then that is how I will spend it. I am sorry for the pain I have caused you. I understand why you left me, and I swear on our child's life that if you give me another chance I will be the husband you deserve, and the husband I should have been from the start if I'd only had the courage to believe what my heart was telling me.'

It felt as if the earth made a full rotation before her beautiful mouth parted.

'I fell in love with you that night too,' she whispered, a dreamy smile playing on her heart-shaped lips. 'When I danced in your arms...it felt as if I'd been dropped into heaven. There were so many times when we were together when I felt that heaven again and being without you...' She sighed and pressed herself closer to him. 'I never wanted to leave you, Giannis. Being without you has been like living with a part of myself missing. You're my life.'

Unable to hold himself back a moment longer, he wrapped his arms around her and pulled her trembling frame tightly to him. 'I love you, Tabitha, with all that I am. Please come back to me.'

Her lips brushed against his throat then inched their way to his mouth. The kiss she bestowed on him was filled with such sweet tenderness that it spoke her answer for her.

Lifting her into his arms, Giannis carried his

wife up the stairs to her bedroom where the passion that had always consumed them came alive once more. But this time it was for ever.

EPILOGUE

THERE WASN'T A cloud in the cobalt Santorini sky. The late-afternoon sun beamed down, its rays matching the rays bursting out of Tabitha's heart.

Giannis's sisters fussed with her hair and her dress. Helena, the fashion designer sister who'd made the alterations needed for the wedding dress to fit Tabitha's post-baby frame, anxiously checked it every five seconds. Katarina, dressed in an identical bridesmaid's dress to her sisters, rocked a fractious baby Elise in her arms, refusing to hand Elise back to Tabitha in case the three-month-old baby was sick on her dress. It was with much relief that Giannis's mother, who was the designated babysitter for the day, returned from greeting the entire extended Basinas family, all squashed like sardines within the confines of the blue-topped church, snatched her newest grandchild into her arms and bustled back inside with her.

The only one of their small party stood on the steps of the church not nervous was Tabitha. She couldn't wait to get in there.

A sharp elbow landed in her ribs. 'Look,' shouted Niki, laughing.

Tabitha followed her gaze and saw a small plane flying over them with her and Giannis's names trailing behind it on a long banner.

She saw something else too that filled her heart with equal joy at this public declaration of her husband's love. The moon had risen on this long summer's day too, as if it had come out early to celebrate with them. She imagined her parents sat on it, watching her. She thought they would approve that this time, the time when the vows she was going to exchange meant everything, she was wearing the wedding dress that had belonged to Elise, her mother. And she thought they would approve of how she had given Brigstock Manor to the local authority to be turned into a children's home.

She blew the moon a kiss, then stepped inside the church to renew her wedding vows to the man who had made her the happiest woman on earth.

* * * * *